Diary of A
13-Year-Old Girl

Bailey Porras

KidPub Press
Boston

Published by KidPub Press
www.kidpub.com

ISBN: 978-1-61018-078-8

Printed in USA

Inspired by life and friends

Thank you, Kuranda, Alex, Natalie, Alexa, Lily, and Sydney!

Thank you Alex and Lily for being a temporary artist!

Thank you Bama Michele and Mom for helping me
open up my mind and write what I feel!

Thank you Bama Joanne and Dad for helping pay for my book to
be published and supporting me every step of the way!

Thank you Sabrina for leaving me alone (some of the time)!

Chapter 1

"**G**ET UP," YELLED SABRINA. "C'MON! You're going to be late for your very first day of school!"

"Ugh," I said while I helplessly rolled out of bed... ever so slowly so I would be late, and my mom hates me being late, so maybe, I would slip out of this one. I look at my huge whiteboard on the side of my wall to look at the date. It was the first day of school. Ugh.

"Finally," moans Sabrina when she sees me fully dressed. "That took you forever!"

Sabrina is my fifteen-year-old sister. I'm thirteen. My other two sisters are twins and their names are Kate and Sarah, both six, and my little brother, Cole, is five. I also have a nineteen-year old brother, Kevin, but no one really sees him because he already went off to college, and he works on the days he's not learning, except for holidays when he comes home. My mom and Dad are somewhere in their forties... but I lost track.

"Does it get any worse?" I silently thought to myself, while walking to school. I was shortly answered by a 'yes' later in the day. Half exited? Yeah, but you know how school is sometimes. (A bore.) So the first thing you do when you get there on your first day of school is find your new desk. Yes, but before that? I know it's sometimes frightening: you meet your new teacher. I happen to have a great teacher, Mrs. Bartelstone, but she says for us to call her plain Mrs. B. I found my nametag, and took my seat between Hayden and nobody.

Almost done with 7th grade, I now sit between Brian and… nobody. There are six people at my table: Brian, Michelle, Ally, Scarlet, Josh, and me. We sit at table number 3, but 2 will always be my favorite number.

On Friday, I'm going to my other friend's house, Kaleen, but we call her KK. Gwen, my other BFF is coming too. Plus Elizabeth, Ally, Scarlet and Nikki, Mattie, JJ (Janette), Bailey and Michelle and a bunch of other friends of Kaleen. (And me!)

Wednesday report: Yes. So far, Wednesday is fine. But that is what I thought before I found out I forgot my homework. My trusty friend, Michelle gave me the problems and I worked them all out just before the bell rang. Saved by Michelle!

Today was league. League is a sport chosen by the teachers, and this time it's tennis baseball. The bell rang, meaning it's time to go home! I rode home on my bike. I pass birds, the creek, people and grass, a bunch of grass. Wow, talk about boredom.

Ten minutes later…

Then, I decided I was really bored, so I went on AOL and checked my email. And, yes. Never fails. Sabrina marches straight into the computer room, and guess what she does? She actually says for me to get off. Wow, I think to myself. Then I say out loud "No way. I just got on. And I've gotta check my email."

"But, I want to check my Facebook. You have been on for, like 10 minutes, and I haven't been on for the whole day! Haylie? Why can't I get on?" Sabrina whines. Before I get to answer, she screams in my face.

Then, I say sarcastically, "Gee, thanks. You are the best sister ever. And no, I'm not getting off," After about a minute of yelling in my face, she gives up. Yay, I think to myself. Finally.

After about fifteen minutes of answering emails, I get bored, so I let Sabrina on.

I go into my room, and slouch down on my bed. I hear a yell for my name. "Haylie," my mom yells. I run into the kitchen, and my mom says, "Haylie. I just got a call from Elizabeth." Elizabeth is my BFF. "She wants to know if you can come over while I go out tonight for Sabrina's conference, but I've already scheduled for Bama to come over and watch you," (Bama is my Grandma. We just call her that because when Sabrina was a baby, my mom said, "Say Grandma," and she always said, "Bama!") "So what do you want to do? Do you want Bama to come stay with you, or do you want to go over to Elizabeth's?"

"Um, Maybe I could go over to Elizabeth's, if that's okay?" I say.

"Sure," she agrees

I slouch down, again, and start reading Melting of the Maggie Bean. I'm really into that serious. I've read Maggie Bean in Love, The Secret Identity of Devon Delaney, and I plan on reading Maggie Bean Stays Afloat next. So, I've pretty much finished that series.

An hour passed. Two. Finally, my mom tells me it's time to go. We hop into my mom's sky blue Bentley. (My mom has a Bentley and my dad has a Porsche convertible.) We turn the street of Stoneshead. I see Elizabeth hopping up and down, trying to grab my attention. I hop out of the car. "Thanks, Mom!" I say. She nods and drives off. We walk up her long, curvy driveway.

"Wanna jump in the pool?" she said.

"Sure, if you want to," It sounded fun. Her pool was pretty good. But I couldn't say I didn't want to, because I really did.

"Okay. Let's go put on our bathing suits!" she says. We run into her two-story house and into her room. When we are finished with putting on our bathing suits, we go down a staircase and outside to her pool. We are pulled in by each other.

"Ahhh!" we scream.

One hour later…

"Elizabeth? That was so much fun! We should do this again."

"Okay. Not tomorrow, I have cheer. Not the next day, I'm going to the zoo Um… how about you just… call me sometime, then?"

"Sounds good," I said. "Well, I've got to go home, now. My mom told me to be home by 5:00."

I really just wanted to see Seth at a pool party, which Seth invited me to. I didn't want to say anything to Elizabeth, because she wasn't very fond of Matt. (More like they were ENEMIES.) On Matt's popular list, she was like 63rd… I'm third, right behind Seth and Matt, of course. I didn't want to tell her that she wasn't invited. I didn't even want to tell her about it. The less she knew, the better. That might sound mean, but let's just say she is REALLY VERY sensitive.

Anyway, her house was like a block away from pool, so it was a short pleasant walk down the HUGE hill of Stoneshead.

So, I walked out of her house, after saying goodbye and thanking her Mom. Down, down, down her curvy driveway. I thought I heard a person following me, but I keep on walking. When I got there, I relaxed and sat on a pool chair. I didn't want to swim; I guess you could say I… wasn't in the mood. So, I called my mom, telling her I saw a few of my friends at the pool, and maybe, with her permission, if I could stop by, blah, blah, blah. Even though I was already there. This was PLANNED.

Suddenly, I hear, "Ouch! Stop! Elizabeth... Umph!" Matt says, beat up. I spin around to see Elizabeth slapping Matt across the face and Matt's spit flying. (Gross) Hahaha. I know it sounds funny, but... okay, it was funny.

"Hey! Elizabeth, what on Earth..." I laugh.

"Um... I... am... not... here. You... do... not... see... me," she tried.

"Elizabeth... we talked about this!" I whisper. "Wait... so you were the one following me here?"

"Um... is that bad?"

"Um, yeah!" Matt says.

Forty-five minutes later, when I found out Elizabeth already knew about the popular list. She said "Matt's list?! Matt's is the last judgment I would care about, IN MY LIFE!!!"

And, I went along with it.

"Guys, I have to go. See you at school," I leave for home.

So, it's, like, 10:00. I'm really tired, and I just finished watching So You Think You Can Dance.

"Mom, I think I'll go to sleep," I told her when she came into my room later that night.

"Okay, honey. See you in the morning," my mom answers.

I slouch down on my bed, and, ever so slowly, I start to drift off to sleep...

Chapter Two

"Haylie!" Sabrina booms. "Haylie, it's Thursday! Wake up! Seriously, c'mon. You're gonna make me late."

"No... too tired... too sleepy..." I say.

"Get up or I'll pour water on you," I knew she would (by experience).

So (already cold) I shoot up, thinking how cold I would be if icy water was poured all over me. "What? What time is it," I ask sleepily.

"It's 7:14."

"Okay, okay," I whimpered. Even though I'm slightly dizzy.

I got up and ate Corn Flakes.

Then, I got dressed: turquoise bracelet, blue tennis shoes, jean shorts, and an Abercrombie and Fitch t-shirt.

I packed my lunch.

I brushed my teeth and combed my hair, and packed my backpack with Science and Social Studies textbooks, my keys to my house, my lunch, and my iPod. I threw my phone into the front pocket of the backpack.

My mom drove my siblings and me to school; Colina was the first stop.

So, I walked up the steps. "Colina Middle School," the sign read. In the distance, I saw two of my closest friends, Scarlet and Ali chatting about something.

I walked up to them. "Hi, guys."

"Hey," Ali responds.

"Hi," says Scarlet. Then they started talking to me.

I interrupted, "I have to go, guys. But see you later? I have to talk to Michelle about homework."

"Okay, bye," says Ali and Scarlet exchanging glances, which probably means they are thinking, "Is this girl crazy? She just got here???"

I run off to my classroom, room sixteen. I see Michelle and take a seat next to her. "Hey," I say.

"Hi. What did you think about our Science project? It's due tomorrow, you know," she fills me in.

"Yeah, I know. I guess it's okay, but that's not what I came to talk about," I tell her.

She puts down her pen, and moves her math paper into her green folder, and into her desk, now looking serious. "Okay. I'm all ears, now. What do you want to talk about?"

"I… forgot my homework again. Do you mind?" I said weakly.

"Okay," she nods her head.

"Thank you so much! It won't happen again."

"You're welcome. I don't care. What are friends for?" she asked.

"Yeah. Thanks."

"Okay, here," she hands me her homework.

"Thanks!" And, I ran to my desk to copy it.

When I was done (ten minutes later), I thanked her; the bell rang, and people filed in, talking, gossiping, and laughing.

I waved to Scarlet, "Hey!" I whispered.

"Hey," she said back. "I forgot my homework! Answers?"

I nod and laugh. "Yeah, I have them," and I told her the story of how I got the answers from Michelle.

She laughed, "Ha! How funny." I handed them over to her. Just as the final bell rang and our teacher, Mr. Burns walks in, she finishes and throws the sheet of paper back to me.

I smiled, and she smiled back.

Class begins…

"Let's see, here. If y=7, what plus y = 18? Easy! 11," I think to myself.

I heard a bell. Oh, good. I think of what to do at recess. I hear another bell. I think of how good it will feel to stuff my Oreo cookie into my mouth! Another bell rings. I think of how amazing it will be when school ends for the day. A fourth bell sounds deafening. I think how good it will feel when school ends for the year.

Then, I hear the class breathe a sigh of relief, and then see them run out the door.

Then I realized it was recess time! (I know it's weird to have recess in middle school. We didn't but the class bet that the Green Bay Packers would beat the Pittsburgh Steelers, and bet recess. So, our class has recess. Mr. Burns set the bell in the office to ring, I guess.) So, I ran out of the classroom and plop myself down on the bench. I run back to the classroom and take out my Oreo cookie I packed myself for snack. Yum!

Then, I plop myself down on the bench, yet again. Just as fast as I sit down, Elizabeth pulls me off to the field even faster. (We have a special field in Colina. "Nose goes!" Scarlet exclaims.

Everyone touches her own nose at practically the same time.

"'Bows goes!" I suggest.

The last person to touch their elbow was Mattie.

We run onto the field.

"HAYLIE!"

It's the very first thing I hear when I try to enjoy myself? That doesn't seem very fair, does it?

I spin around and see Seth.

"Haylie! Incoming!!"

Oh my gosh. Right there running at an uncontrollable speed straight at me, is Seth. Oh my gosh!

Seth or no Seth, I would rather have NO ONE running at me.

BAAAAMM!

"Ouch!" I say, clutching my arm. I realized Seth had run into me.

Kaleen was rubbing her elbow, too, and I realized, actually, that Seth had run into Kaleen, who had run into me. And it HURT!

"Haylie? Kaleen? Oh my gosh… I'm so… are you guys okay?" he says.

"No. I think they're still alive," says Josh slapping Drake a high-five.

"No duh," Seth laughs.

"Yeah. I'm fine, I guess. You could've given me some kind of warning, though," I said, kicking Kaleen in the shin, motioning to PLAY ALONG.

"Yeah! Gosh, Seth," she said, and frowned.

I gave her a thumbs-up.

"I did! Oh my gosh! I'm so…"

We smile and laugh.

"Hey!" he laughs.

Kaleen slaps me a high-five, and all the girls laugh hysterically.

Chapter Three

I T'S FRIDAY. IN ENGLISH CLASS, I am reading.

I flipped the 216th page of the new book I'm reading, Middle school: how to deal.

Kaleen passed a note to me.

Hey! So bored!

I wrote:

Hey. I'm super bored, too.

Ha! So, what do you wanna talk about?

I dunno. Who do you like?

Don't you already know?

No.

Really?!

Yeah.

Oh. I like Josh.

JOSH!!! Ewww.

Hey!

Sorry, I just never thought that ANYONE would like him. I... let's just say I don't think he's...very cute.

Oh no! Mr. Burns alert! STOP PASSING NOTES NOW! He'll see!

I nodded and laughed.

Soon, the bell rang. So, I closed the book, slid it into my desk, bolted out of my seat, and sprinted to the cafeteria. I sat down next to Elizabeth and Gwen. I realized I left my lunch back in class.

I got up and ran back to room sixteen.

When I turned the corner, I was greeted with another bang into Ali.

I studied her.

She had my lunch box.

"Here," she laughed. "You forgot this back at the classroom."

"Thanks," I blushed with embarrassment.

I turned to leave.

"Oh, wait! I was wondering if you could go to hang at Yozo Frozo," (Yozen Frogurt. She always calls it Yozo Frozo.) "Kaleen, Elizabeth, Nikki, Natalie, and Scarlet are going."

"Oh, frozen yogurt is great! Thanks for the invite. I'll be there!"

"Yeah, okay. See you there."

"Okay. Bye!" I said.

"But… make sure not to invite anyone extra… I don't want it to turn into a huge thing."

"Okay," I said. "So… wanna sit with me at lunch?"

"Yeah."

And, we walked to the cafeteria together.

I was talking to Kaleen, Ali, and Elizabeth when…

CRASH! "OUCH!"

I turned around only to see my twin six-year-old sisters lying on the ground.

Chapter Four

"OH MY GOSH! SARAH! KATE! Why are you here? How did you…" I was baffled. I started asking questions rapidly. I rushed over to them and took Kate in my arms and Sarah held my hand. I ran to Mrs. Bartelstone's room. "Guys, wait here," I sit them down by the door of Mrs. Bartelstone's room. "Excuse me, Mrs. B," I ask. "May I be excused? I just found my little sisters at the school."

"Um, okay…" She says. "Why are they…?"

"I don't really know."

There was a silence.

"Would you like a ride? We still have 25 minutes until lunch ends. I could drive you home," she offers.

"Thanks but no thanks. It's not that far from here to my house."

"Okay, Haylie. You are excused from homework. Are you sure you don't want me to call your Mom?" she picked up the phone.

"Oh, I'm sure! I'll call her from my cell. Thanks, Mrs. B!" I ran out the door and grabbed Sarah and Kate's hands.

"Come on, Kate," I said. She was kind of trailing behind. It was a little less than a quarter-of-a-mile to my house. We crossed a few streets and had a few close calls.

When I got home, I yelled into the house, "Mom! Why did I just find Sarah and Kate in my school cafeteria?" There was no reply. "Mom? Mom! Hello!?" still no reply. I call my mom's cell phone. Voice message. "Hi, it's Stephanie. I can't take your call right now, but if you leave a brief message stating your name and number, I'll get back to you as soon as possible. Thank you," Beep.

"Hi, Mom. It's me, Haylie. I was excused from school because Sarah and Kate were found in my school cafeteria. I'm calling from the home phone. Um, call me back at the home number. I definitely can't handle these kids. I wish you'd come home! Sarah's already crying! I should go. No Sarah! Stop! Don't you dare! Kate! STOP THAT!!! If you don't stop... bye, Mom!"

I hung up the phone. I started to relax then I thought of what to do next. I think... I know! I could call Sabrina! Wow, I'm good!

I spin around just in time to see the phone base crash on the floor and to see Kate weeping about her bloody knee and to see Sarah screaming, "I didn't do it! I'm innocent!"

"UGH! SARAH! KATE! You are in so much..." I scream.

"Oh, wow. I'm really sorry, guys," I apologized. "Why don't we walk down the block and get us some Yozen Frogurt?" We live around the corner to a shopping center.

"You don't deserve yogurt!" Sarah says.

"Yeah!" Kate agrees. "You yelled at us!"

"You're right. I don't. But you do. How about this: I'll walk you guys down there and you can choose any flavor you want? And I don't have any for myself? How's that?" I ask.

They think for a minute. Then, Kate says, "Sarah! Private meeting! Now! In my bedroom."

"You mean our bedroom. We share one!" says Sarah.

"Yeah," Kate burns bright red. She blushes, "That's what I said," They ran off. I waited for them to come back.

"Okay," says Kate. "Okay, we will accept your offer."

"Thank you," I say even though I have no clue in the world why I'm thanking them.

We walked down to the corner of our street and Sarah screams, "Hey, Haylie!"

"Yes?" I ask.

"Haylie! There's spider on you!" I look onto my pant legs. No spider. "It's on your shirt!" I look onto my shirt. No spider. "It's on your…"

"Just stop, Sarah. There is no spider on me."

"No, really! There is a spider, possibly a black widow, on your arm!"

"Okay," I laugh. "Okay, I'll look on my arm for the spider," I was sure there was no spider. I look onto my arm. There, sure enough is a spider. A house spider, but, still, it's a spider.

"Oh, great!" I brush off my arm sending the spider flying. "Let's get going," We head down the corner and then to the ice cream store.

"Oh, no," I saw Kaleen and Gwen fighting.

"Uh, guys, come on in…"

"Hey! There's Elizabeth! Can we say hi?!" Kate asked.

They loved Elizabeth because she was always nice to kids, especially them.

"I don't see why not," I said, and opened the door.

We walked into Yozen Frogurt (Yozo Frozo), and Elizabeth squealed, "Hi guys!!!" And ran over to Kate and Sarah.

"Hi, Elizabeth!!!" Sarah exclaimed.

They got their own table.

"Uh… hey Elizabeth…" I said.

"Oh! Sorry, Haylie!"

"It's okay," I giggled.

She went back to her table with Sarah and Kate.

"Haylie!" Ali exclaimed.

"Hi!"

"Come here!" Kaleen exclaimed from the table everyone was sitting at. "Take a seat!"

"Okay," I shrugged and walked over. I took the last spot in between Kaleen and Ali. Elizabeth rushed over.

"Sorry. I'll sit," and she left Kate and Sarah with a couple of cheap, plastic dolls.

"Thank you for giving them… presents. It'll keep 'em busy!" I exclaimed.

Everyone laughed.

After we talked for a while, I said, "I think I'm going to go order."

"Can I make a suggestion?" Scarlet asked.

I shrugged.

"Irish Mint!" She exclaimed.

"No way! Chocolate!" Shouted Natalie.

"Go with hazelnut," Nikki said plainly.

"Okay…" I walked away, laughing.

"Guys!" I said to Kate and Sarah. "Come on! Let's order."

"Okay," Sarah said.

So, I get a cup (it's self-serve at Yozen Frogurt) and grab one for Kate and Sarah.

"Wait," I hear Sarah say. "Wait, Haylie! I changed my mind. I think you deserve a yogurt."

"Oh. Why the sudden change of mind?"

"I dunno. Because you are buying us some."

"Oh! So, I can get a yogurt, then?"

"Yes, you can," Kate nods.

"Cool."

We all get our flavors and step up in line to get our yogurts weighed. (I got Irish mint and red velvet cake mixed. Sarah got chocolate and vanilla mixed. Kate got Butterfinger and red velvet.) When we are done, Sarah says, "Okay. Thanks, Haylie."

"Yeah!" exclaimed Kate.

"Welcome," I smiled.

I heard a familiar ring tone, and then I notice it's mine. "Why don't you guys go to our table and eat your ice cream?"

I took a spoonful of mine. Mmmmm!

"Okay," says Sarah.

"Hello?" I said into the phone.

"Hi, honey," I hear Mom saying. "I got your message and I've been texting you for some time, now."

"Oh, sorry, Mom. I guess I didn't notice! Call you back, bye!"

"No, Haylie, wait. What's this about Kate and Sarah being found in your school cafeteria?"

"Oh, Mom, I don't know," I took another bite. "I found them right there lying on the ground. I still haven't asked them why. We've been too busy…"

"You've been too busy doing what?"

I took another bite. "Um," I said. "Mom…"

"Honey, where are you?"

"Mom. We are all at Yozen Frogurt. I bought yogurt for us," And another bite.

"Sweetie," she explains. "Sweetie, it's fine. Just, please plan on telling me before you go somewhere while alone in the house. And it was very nice of you to spend your own money on treats for your sisters and you."

"Okay, Mom. Will do. We'll be back home in 5 minutes, okay?"

"Oh, honey. I appreciate it, but there's no rush! I'll be home in two hours! Isn't that plenty of time to 'chill', as you kids say, nowadays?"

"First of all: we never say 'chill'."

"Hey. Haylie, play nice."

"Okay, sorry Mom."

"Okay. Love you!" I hear a kissing sound.

"Ew, Mom!"

She giggled and hangs up.

Twenty minutes later, I decided I should go home so I could finish my homework.

"Bye!!!" I said to the girls at Yozen.

And we started home.

Chapter Five

"**O**KAY," WE WALKED INTO OUR house. "Now, first things first. What I want you guys to do is sit down, do your homework, and then clean up the mess you made in the kitchen with the phone. Since there's no glass, pick the cord off the floor... and all the pieces of... what was the phone... and put them on the counter, okay?"

"Okay," Sarah says, snickering.

"With my supervision," I tell them.

"Dang it!" Kate stomped.

"Unless I can trust you alone."

"You can. I'll watch Kate," Sarah said. (The good child...)

I smile. I sit on a chair in the kitchen and take out my iPod. "You guys just go ahead and do your homework while I listen to music, okay?"

"But, what if we ever need help? Would you help us?"

"Yes, Sarah."

"Okay."

I led them to the "Study Room". It's the room where we study and do homework. I make sure they are separated so that Kate doesn't copy off of Sarah's paper, even though it's just a drawing for Kindergarten. They might have a fight, anyway.

Having known that Kate and Sarah were occupied, I dashed upstairs into my bedroom, flopped onto my bed, and snatched my phone from my back pocket to call Mom. I waited for the dial tone and dialed her number. When there was no answer, I decided to text wildly. I texted her once and waited. Twice then waited. And then decided to call her, again. "Hello?" she answered.

"Oh hi, Mom. I'm so glad you answered! I'm at home with Kate and Sarah. They are working on their homework."

"Oh, that's great, honey! But, you do know that they might... they will need your help with homework."

"Yeah, Mom. I told them if they need help, I would help them. But... I don't think they will: it's just a drawing. And... while we're talking, I wanted to run something by you," I say without giving her time to respond. "I was thinking, and you know how I'm always asking you for things and you sometimes say that I should get a job to make some money?"

"Yes. And you should. I'm not just saying this for no reason!"

"I know, Mom, I know. So what I was thinking of was maybe my new job for the summer or whenever could be pet sitting," I say. "Wait! Before you say no, please, please, please!"

"Um, honey..."

"Mom. I could..."

"Honey, let me talk!"

"Okay. Sorry, Mom."

"Okay, so pet sitting, huh? Well, I think that's a great idea!"

"So, yes? Yes I can pet sit," I squeal.

"Yes. Honey, listen to me. With watching pets comes lots of responsibility. You have to walk, feed, and play with them. And it won't be an easy task. Also, care for them. And if you were supposed to visit the pet and you just forget, you lose the job, basically. It's a hard job. But, if you are up to it, then you can do it. Only for the neighbors, though, okay?"

"Neighbors, why only for the neighbors?"

"Well, honey. Let's say you have a job all the way in Irvine. Or Moorpark. Or on a different cul-de-sac. I can't drive you to all of them. So it'll have to be on this cul-de-sac and the next over on each side, okay?"

"Okay, Mom."

"Good for you! You got a job!"

I hear a voice in the background. "Um," it's saying. "Mrs. Carter?"

"Yes?" my mother answers.

"You're up next."

"Okay. Honey? I have to go. I'm up next."

"Where are you, anyway?"

"I'm at an interview, honey."

"Okay then, Mom. See you in an hour. Oh, and good luck!!!" I hung up the phone. Then, I walked to the door to go downstairs to see how Kate and Sarah are doing. "Oh my gosh! Sarah? Kate? How long have you been standing there?" I see Sarah and Kate standing on the other side of my door listening to my conversation with Mom.

"Three, four minutes," Sarah hesitates. "If my calculations are correct."

"So for the whole time we've been home, you've accomplished nothing. No homework, no cleaning, nothing."

"Yep. Pretty much," Sarah rolls her eyes. "Wow, it takes you an eternity to catch on!"

"I am very disappointed in you guys. You were eavesdropping instead of doing homework or cleaning or… oh, no! I'm starting to sound like Mom!"

"Yes you are!"

"Thanks, Kate. Thanks for your honest opinion."

"Oh, it's not an opinion," she laughs. "It's the truth."

"Ha, ha, ha. Very funny," I say sarcastically.

"That's why I'm laughing."

"Okay," I think out loud. "This time, I'll be in the same room as you when you are doing your homework. That way, you won't fool around again. But if I get up to do something and I come back and see you doing anything else then homework, you will be in a lot of trouble, got that?"

"Yeah. Got it," Kate answers.

"Fine. Follow me," We walked down the hall into the Study Room. "Tell me if you ever need help."

My phone vibrates. "Hello?" I say into the phone. "Hello," I hear someone say.

"Guess who?"

"I have no idea. You got me. Who?"

"Haylie. It's Elizabeth."

"Oh, Beth. Hi. What's up?" (I call her Beth all the time.)

"So are you going to the dance tomorrow night?"

"Oh. Um… I guess. I'd have to ask my mom, first, okay?"

"Okay! So maybe see you there?"

"Yeah," I said.

There is a Moment of silence.

"So, I gotta go. I'm alone with my sisters."

"Oh, yeah. You found your sisters at school!" She said.

"Yeah."

"I don't mean to invite myself, but maybe I could come over and help you, I you need help," she volunteers.

"Okay, yeah! Lemme call and ask my mom, first."

I rushed upstairs and (once again) snatch my phone from my back pocket, wait for the dial tone and dial Mom's cell phone number. "Hello?" she answers the phone.

"Mom! Um, I just got a phone call."

"Uh huh."

"And it was from Elizabeth."

"Uh huh."

"And she told me that there was this dance."

"Uh huh."

"It's really close by."

"Uh huh."

"And it's totally casual and everything. It's tomorrow."

"Uh huh."

"And she asked me if I was going."

There was a long pause.

"Uh huh. Honey, would you be going alone?!"

"Yeah. But it's casual and it's nothing big and there will be tons of other kids, you know?"

"Do you want to go?"

"Yeah, of course. And it won't be long. It's totally casual!" I throw in again.

"Okay, Haylie. Go. Have fun. But be home by 8:00."

"Mom."

"8:30?"

"Mom," I said, wanting her to go higher.

"9:30?" she said.

"Good. I'll be home by 9:30, okay?"

"Sounds good! Bye."

"Wait, Mom?"

"Huh?"

"When will you be home?"

"I'm just getting into the car."

"Oh. So Elizabeth can't come over?"

"Well…"

"Please!" I said.

"Okay, but only for about two hours, okay?"

"Okay, thanks Mom!" I pressed the end button.

"Sarah! Kate!"

"Yeah?"

"Come up here… quick!"

"Coming… whoa! Ouch!" One of them said. I couldn't tell who, because they sound almost as identical as they look.

"Are you okay?"

"No. I think I broke it! It hurts," she sobs. It was Sarah. It was definitely Sarah.

"Wait. Hold on, Sarah. Broke what? What hurts?"

"My leg!!!!!"

"Hold on, Sarah. I'm coming," I race to the staircase to see Sarah crying and Kate trying to comfort her. "Sarah. Tell me everything that happened in order from start to finish."

"Well," she sobs, "I was coming up the stairs when you called me, and I slipped. When Kate tried to catch me, she fell on top of me and I tumbled down the staircase. And then you asked me what happened, and now I'm telling you the story."

"Okay, and did you land on your leg?"

"No, Kate did."

I glanced at Kate to see her guilty look. "I'm sorry, Sarah," she shuffles her feet. "I didn't mean to hurt you. Please don't be mad at me."

"I'm not mad, Kate. Just be careful, okay?"

Her face brightens.

"Sarah," I say. "Come here. You too, Kate," I lead them into the kitchen, carrying Sarah. When we reached the kitchen, I told them to sit down.

I was going to tell them about the dance. It was important that I told them because some nights, they wanted me to stay home and play stupid board games.

"Guys, you know how I'm older, now and I can do a lot of things?"

They nod.

"Well, you know Elizabeth?"

They nod. "I love Elizabeth!" Kate said.

"Anyway, she called about ten minutes ago," I pause and then open the freezer door to get Sarah an icepack. "Um, she told me about this dance…" I walk over to Sarah and give her the icepack. She looks at me and (suspiciously) rests it on her leg.

Well, I'm going to a dance tomorrow night. Is that okay?"

They took a Moment to hesitate.

"Fine… I think."

"Think?"

"Yeah," said Sarah. "I might have something planned."

"Um… okay… well, thanks for approving!!!"

They stared at me.

Ding-dong. I hear the doorbell ring. "That must be Mom. Kate, go get it, please."

She runs to the door and opens it. "Hi, Mommy!" I hear her say. "I missed you!"

"I know, honey. I missed you, too. Where are Sarah and Haylie?"

"In the kitchen, Mom," I yell.

She then comes into view. "Hi, Mom. Did you get the job?"

"Oh, honey, I don't know. I have to wait a week to find out. But... Sarah! What happened to your poor leg?"

"I fell down the staircase, Mommy. Sorry if I got blood on the stairs."

"Oh, honey. All that matters is that you're okay. Are you?"

"Yes, Mommy. At first, I thought I broke it, but I realized it was either sprained or just plain hurt."

"Good, honey. Not that you hurt your leg, but it's not broken. That's good."

"Yep."

"Girls, did you finish your homework?"

There was a long silence.

"Um... yeah, Mom they did," I say, even though they didn't.

"Well, then, Kate and Sarah? Can I see it?" she beat the lie with one small question.

"Um..." Kate panics.

"Yes, you can. Kate, can you come here," I tell her that she and Sarah could do their homework while I'm talking to Mom. She agreed to the plan. She then told Sarah.

"Girls. Can I see your homework?" Mom asks impatiently.

"Yeah, Mom. Let them look for it, first," I covered for them.

"You lost your homework? Let me look for it with you."

"No, Mom. We have to talk. Let them look."

"Wait," Sarah cuts in. "We just have to write our name on it, then you can see it."

"Well, okay. Go on, then," she believes the lie.

They jump up from their chair (Kate walking, Sarah limping), and Mom and

I wait until I can't see them anymore.

"So, Mom. About Elizabeth coming over... I... I'm too lazy to call her myself. Can you call her Mom and see if she can come over?"

"Um, okay," she shrugged.

After she was finished talking to Elizabeth's Mom, I talked to Elizabeth about the dance. Our Moms decided we were going together. We lived a few streets over from each other.

"So..." She said. "When should we leave?"

"At 9:15," I inform her.

"When should we leave for the dance?"

"5:30."

"Okay. What should we bring," she asks.

"I'll bring salad... you bring finger sandwiches."

"And how do we get home?"

"Maybe one of our parents can drive us back," I say.

"I volunteer my mom," she said.

"Okay. Um... I guess I'll see you."

"Yeah," she says. "I'll see you tomorrow," she hangs up the phone.

Chapter Six

S O, IT'S SATURDAY, THE NIGHT of the dance. "Wow, I slept in," I said. The clock said 11:47. Not that I needed to get up, I mean it's a Saturday. I walked downstairs lazily seeing my mom, my dad, Cole, Kate and Sarah eating together. "Hi," I say sheepishly. "Why didn't you wake me?"

"Well," my dad tells me, "it's bad luck to wake a late sleeper!"

I smile. "That's still no excuse!" I walk up to the counter and grab an apple, a piece of bacon, and a half a bagel. "Yum," I take a bite of bacon, "Who made this bacon?"

"Your sisters," my mom replies.

"Oh. Good job," I smile.

"Thank you," Kate said acknowledging her cooking abilities. I nodded. I walked to the refrigerator door and pulled out the cream cheese. I sat down at the table and spread just enough cream cheese to make a girl's mouth water. I took a bite. "This is good. Who made this?" I comment. It was weird: homemade cream cheese, but it did taste pretty good.

"Me," Cole stepped forward.

"Good job," I picked him up, hugged him, and set him back down. The whole family started pigging out. When finished with my bacon, I devoured my bagel and ate half of my apple.

"Don't fill up yet!" My mom takes a platter and sets it in front of me. I look over it. "Eggs," I say. "Who made these? Wait let me guess. Cole, Kate, or Sarah."

"Actually," my mom corrects me, "I did."

"Oh. Good job, Mom," I compliment after filling my plate with eggs.

About ten minutes later, the whole family is finished. "Good breakfast," I say cheerfully. "I have to go… do some stuff, so bye!"

"Wait!" Cole grabs my hand. "Whoa, Cole?" I stumbled backward trying not to slip and fall.

"Love you, Haylie."

"Cole, I'm only going upstairs into my room."

"I know. Can I come?" his face brightens.

"No!"

"Anyway, Cole," she interrupts, "I have an extra job for you. Haylie needs some alone time, okay?"

"Okay," he groans.

I mouth the words thank you to my mom and dash upstairs. I wanted to call around and see just how many people I knew were going to the dance. I punched in Elizabeth's number. Voice message. Kaleen: voice message. Nikki: voice message. I called three more people, and still: voice message. I walk into the office and slouch down on the chair and pull up to the computer. I check my email and my IM. "You've got mail," the computer tells me. I check and I had not one, but eighteen new emails. I checked a few of them.

Some were talking about how cool the dance was going to be.

The rest are commenting on my Facebook wall, saying hi, and seeing me at the dance, or asking if we could hang out. I sigh, and press the escape button. I walked away from the computer. By this time, it's almost 1:00. I decided I'd better make that salad I had promised Elizabeth, so I made a big bowl of chicken Caesar salad with croutons. Yum, my mouth waters. This'll be good, so, I cover it with plastic wrap and place in the refrigerator.

I decide to choose my dress, shoes, and accessories now. So, I walk up the staircase and into my room. I open my walk-in-closet and pull out four dresses: A purple velvet short dress, a short black wrap, a satin gray short dress, and a short hot pink dress.

The purple velvet: love the length but I hate the fuzz. It looks too little weird for me. That dress is a no. Actually, I don't even know why I still have that! I thought I threw it out a month ago! I threw it in a brown box titled GIVE AWAYS. Gray satin: looks weird with my skin tone and hair. Nope. Short black wrap: cute, but the pink one was better!

I picked the pink one. I laid it down on my bed with a pair of black flats and a black headband. "Cute," my mom acknowledges from the door. I turn around. "Thanks."

"You're welcome. Don't you want something to eat before you go?"

"Yes please!"

"What do you want?" she asks.

"Hmm. What should I have?"

"What do you want?"

"I don't know," I sat down on a chair.

"You love burgers," she suggested.

"Mmm. Sounds great!"

"Oh, and Mom?"

"Yes, honey?"

"No rush on that cheeseburger. I still have hours."

"Okay."

I closed the door again. I lie back on my bed and pick up my book, The Girl Who Could Fly. It's a great book about, well, a girl who could fly. The title says it all!

When I was halfway finished with chapter fourteen, my mom called me downstairs. My burger was ready. So, I walked downstairs and into the kitchen.

"Hi, honey. Your food is ready."

"Thanks," walking over to the counter, I lick my lips. "This looks really good."

"Really," she asked. "I decided to make them for the whole family for dinner, tonight. Taste it," she urged.

"I will," And I did. "Yum. Mom, this is awesome!" Well, my dad owned a restaurant and taught Mom all of his secrets.

"Are you sure?" her face puzzled and her forehead crinkled up. I nodded. She said, "That's a store-bought cheeseburger. I didn't even add anything to it."

"Well, it's good," I stood by my opinion.

"Well, I better go and do some work," My mom always has worked from home. "And take some calls," she sells houses. You guessed it: she's a realtor. (She was at a work interview because she's looking for a better job that she likes.)

"Mom, wait. What time is it," I ask.

"Oh, almost 2:00."

"Okay. Thanks," I still had three hours and thirty minutes. Cool.

A little while later when I'm finished with my burger…

"Haylie!" Sidney calls. Sidney is Kate's friend. Sarah thought it wasn't fair that Kate got a friend to come over and she didn't have a friend, so she invited Catherine, her best friend since preschool. (Or, as she calls it, BFSP.) Cole complained that he thought it wasn't fair that Catherine and Sidney were over and Mark wasn't, so he talked Mom into letting him over.

"Hi, Sidney! It's been so long since I've seen you!" I say.

"Hi, Haylie," Mark and Catherine said.

"Hi, guys!"

"Come on, Catherine," Sarah said. "Let's go into my room."

"Aw, but I want to stay here and play with Haylie."

"Me? Why?" I ask her.

"Me too!" Mark and Sidney echoed.

"Sarah, if they want to stay here, just let them."

"Fine," she sounded annoyed. I told the same thing to Kate and Cole. "Guys," I explained to them, "why don't you go play. Sidney, go with Kate; Catherine go with Sarah; and Mark go with Cole?"

"Because we want to play with you!" Mark exclaimed.

"Me? You came here to play with Cole."

"I know, but you're funner."

"More fun, you mean."

"Yeah. More fun."

"But, I have to go to a dance with my friends."

"Oooo. Ya gotta crush," Sarah cuts in.

"Hey."

"Do you have a crush on me?" Mark asked suddenly and hopefully.

"Um, no. We're eight years apart. But I think you're cute!"

"Thanks. I know."

"I can't play with you guys because I have to get dressed, brush my hair out, style my hair, pack up my salad, do my makeup, say goodbye to everyone, make sure everything is how it should be and, finally, walk to the dance. I'm really busy!"

"Do you want me to play with Cole?" Mark asks, curiously.

"Please do."

"Fine. I will," so Sarah, Kate, Cole, Mark, Catherine, and Sidney left the kitchen. "Whew," I wondered what time it was. I glanced at the clock. 2:27. Great, I still had hours to spare. So, I went into my bathroom (I have one inside my room). I closed the door. I got out the curler, unwrapped it, and plugged it in. Of course, it did need time to heat up, so I got out the brush and brushed out my hair. I got out some eye shadow and mascara and other makeup supplies. When I was done with my makeup, I checked the iron. It was ready. I took a strand of my hair and brushed it out and curled it. I took another piece and curled it. And another, and another... and so on. When that was over, I walked into my room and collapsed onto my bed. Even though I'm a girl, that was tiring. I decided to watch a movie. I looked through my bookcase and pulled out The Princess Bride. That was a great movie, so I didn't mind watching it again... and again... and again. So, I pressed the "on" button on the remote, and opened the DVD player. Then I inserted the DVD. Okay. I'll get some popcorn, I decided. I walked back downstairs and into the kitchen. "Mom," I call, "I'm making popcorn. Want some?"

"Oh, no thanks. I've had enough. Thanks anyway!"

"I do," the six children exclaimed, loud enough to break windows.

"Um, okay. I'll make four bowls, that way two of you can share one bowl, and I still get one," They nodded their heads and evacuated the room, quietly. So, I ended up making four bowls, instead of one, for the six kids and then, me. I walked the bowls down the hall and opened the door to Cole's room. "Hi, guys. Here's your popcorn."

"Thanks, Haylie. You're the best sister ever!"

I nodded my head. "I know," I walked back down the hall, upstairs and into Kate and Sarah's room.

"Guys! Here," I handed them their popcorn bowls.

"Thank you."

"You're welcome," I left them with a smile, but I was really thinking, I wonder what time it is. I wonder if that cost me so much time that I'm late? So, I looked up at the clock. "3:01," I said aloud. Wow. That coasted me almost no time at all! I still have almost two-and-a-half hours! My cell phone rings. "Hello," I say wondering who could possibly be calling.

"Hi," a woman shrills. "I heard that you were open for pet sitting jobs. Is this true?"

"Yes."

"I am going out of town in ten minutes. Would you watch my two dogs, Marla and Artist?"

"Um, sure. Should I…" I was cut off.

"I'll leave the details on your porch."

"Um, okay. Bye," That was really weird. Mrs. Sweetly is nice and sweet and all, but she's a little (a lot) odd. Five minutes later, I went out onto my front porch and, sure enough, there was a paper attached to a paper, both bright silver colored. When I finished looking over them, I told my mom. Then, I went across the street to Mrs. Sweetly's driveway. Her real name was Mrs. Stanley, but she earned the nickname Mrs. Sweetly. When I entered the house, I fed and patted the dogs, then gave them water, then let them out to go to the bathroom, and finally, played with them and walked them.

Then, when everything was finished and the dogs were back where I left them, I left. I checked my phone to look at the time. 3:42, it read. That left me with plenty of time, still. In fact, it left me with almost one hour and forty-five minutes. Good. Now, I have some time to kill. I ended up not watching the movie. I was tired. Instead I decided to take an hour nap. What? I need sleep and energy, don't I? So, I headed back to my house and into my room. Quietly, I collapsed onto my bed and groaned. My stomached was aching! I then decided that my nap would take my mind off of it. So, I fell asleep by thinking I wouldn't think of the pain if I were asleep. That seemed to make me close my eyes and rest!

Chapter Seven

Wᴴᴇɴ I ᴀᴡᴏᴋᴇ...

I woke up, suddenly. I looked at my clock and read the time. My eyes widened, Five seventeen! Oh, no! I had slept in! I dashed out of bed. "Mom!" I yelled. "Why didn't you wake me up? I over slept! I'm gonna be late!"

"I'm sorry, honey, but I was working. I didn't even know you were sleeping."

I sighed and blew the hair out of my face. I closed the door and changed from my Old Navy shorts and my Abercrombie & Fitch shirt and black tennis shoes into my pink dress and black flats, slipped on my black headband and ran downstairs. "Wait. Mom?"

"Yes, honey?"

"Is my hair still curly?"

"Come here," I went into Mom's workroom. She inspected my hair. "Yes, it's fine."

"Okay," I stopped and glanced at the clock. "Mom! It's almost 5:30. I have to go," I grabbed my salad dish out of the fridge.

"Okay, honey. Have a nice time. And Mrs. Campbell is taking you home?"

"Yes, Mom," Kate and Sarah ran up to hug me. I gave them each a hug. Next came Mark, Cole and Catherine. I gave them hugs. Next: Sidney. I gave her a hug, too. "I love you!" I yell. I closed the door behind me.

Fifteen minutes later…

Elizabeth and I walked in.

"Haylie! Hi. Glad you could make it," Alex yells over the blasting, blaring music.

Elizabeth waved. Alex was her all-time crush.

"Alex. Good to see you, too," I set my salad tray down on a snack table while Matt set down his finger sandwiches. Alex was the guy who pretty much had had a crush on Elizabeth forever! I walked away with Elizabeth.

"So you said everyone would be here. Is anyone even here that I know?"

"Yeah! There's me, Bailey, Nikki, JJ, Kaleen, Scarlet, Gwen, Michelle, Mattie, Jake, Alex, Dean, Jade, Chloe, Michael, Brendan, Seth, Drake, me, you… and do ya know Randal?"

"Wait. Did you say Brendan?"

"Yep," she says.

"Seth?"

"Uh huh."

"And you said Drake, right?"

She nodded.

"Ugh."

"So come on! Let's dance!"

We go onto the dance floor where a group of girls are.

"Hey!" I said. We walked past a few people before we reached the girls. We talked for a minute.

I wanted to check back home. I flipped open my phone and punch in my home number. "Hello?" I hear a voice at the other end of the line.

"Hi, Mom. Um, it's 6:13 right now, and I want you to know that I'm coming home soon."

"That's great, honey. Why did you call, though? Are you lonely?"

"No, Mom. I'm fine, trust me."

"Okay, good. Just tell me if you're ever lonely… hold on."

"Mom? Mom. Hello?"

"Sorry, honey. Cole wants to talk to you. I guess he had some kind of family fun night planned for us, and he refuses to go through with it unless you're here. Talk to him, work it out, tell him that maybe tomorrow we can play together; you know, as a family, all that good stuff to make him feel better. Oh, here he is, now. Say 'hi', Cole!"

"Hi, Haylie."

"Hi, Cole. How are you doing?"

"Good. I'm sad, though."

"Sad? You just said you were doing well. What are you sad about? Wait. Let me guess. You had a family fun night all set up for us and I'm not there with you, so we can't have a family fun night tonight."

"Yeah! What are you, a wizard?"

"No, but a little birdie told me," I see Matt coming back with a grin. "Um, Cole?"

"Yeah?"

"Can you hold on?"

"Yeah," he answers.

"Matt," I say making sure I was covering up the phone so Cole couldn't hear anything. "What'd they say?"

"Nothing, just stuff."

"Stuff?"

"Yeah. Nothing important."

"Tell me, Matt!"

"No. It doesn't really concern you."

"Matt, tell me, now."

"Nope," he says.

"Fine, Matt. You just lost you're date," As I walk away, I put the phone next to my ear, again. "Hi, Cole."

"Hi. I have to put on my pajamas, but I love you," he says.

"Love you," I sighed.

"How," Mom asks, "did you do it?"

"Mom, I honestly don't know. I said a little birdie told me all about his family fun night, asked him how he was doing, and we hung up. That's basically it."

"Well, apparently you did a good job," she paused. "Kate and Sarah want to talk to you. Okay, I'm putting you on speaker."

"Hi," Kate and Sarah say together.

"Hi, Kate. Hi, Sarah. How are you doing?" They sounded pretty occupied.

"Good."

"What're you doing?"

"Watching TV," Faith told me.

"Oh. What are you watching?"

"Wizards of Waverly Place," Sarah says. Go figure. I heard Selena Gomez's voice in the background.

"Cool. I'll be home soon, okay?"

"Okay. Bye!"

"Wait!"

"Yes?"

"Tell Mom I'll be home soon; I love her, and I have to go," I say watching Seth wave at me.

"Okay," Kate agrees.

I hang up the phone. "Seth. What were you guys saying over there?"

"Just talking," he insists.

"About…?"

"Guy stuff."

"Like crushes?"

"Yeah, I guess you could say that," He says coolly.

I opened my mouth to talk and…

"Haylie!"

"Huh," I spun around to see Elizabeth, Nikki, Kaleen, and Bailey.

"I didn't know you were here. I looked everywhere for you," Nikki tells me.

"Oh, well here I am," I say.

"Here you are," she looks confused. "Wait. Are you guys…?"

"No!" Seth says. "We're friends. Just friends."

"Oh," Kaleen says, "I stand corrected."

There was an awkward silence. "So," I say to change the subject and break the silence. "When did you guys get here?"

Seth waved to me and walked away. I waved back.

"Oh," Kaleen says. "I was here at 6:00."

"I was here at 6:00, too," Bailey tells me. "Kaleen and I came together."

"I got here at 6:10 or so," Elizabeth says.

"And I came here at... maybe 5:00," Nikki says.

My eyes widen. "Wow. You got here really early."

"That's because I had to. There was only like ten people here, so the party hadn't started yet, but my mom made this party happen, so we had to set up, pay for food and double, and then triple check our guest list. It was hard work," she replied. She was always the bragging type.

"I can't imagine. At that time, I was still watching my sisters!" I comment.

"You mean Kate and Sarah?" Bailey asks. "I love them! They're the cutest things! How old are they, now?"

The reason Bailey asked that is because she and I aren't really friends, anymore. It's been a long time since she's seen my house or my family, but she sees me every day at school. I think she wants to be friends again. No way that's going to happen. Once you're her friend, she never stops texting you. Or, if you don't have a phone, she buys you one and then she starts texting you constantly. She's really rich. With her, you just can't win.

"Oh, um six," I say.

"Oh. Last time I saw them, they were four, I think. And Cole was... three."

"Yep," I agreed.

"Hay Hay?" she asks. That's my used-to-be nickname she gave me. "I should come over sometime," she invites herself. "It's been, like forever, huh?"

"Yeah. Forever," I see Nikki, Kaleen, and Elizabeth staring at me like they're paralyzed, or something.

"Um, Kaleen?"

"Huh," she sounds surprised.

"Wanna walk around and talk and gossip?" I ask hopefully.

"Yeah," Nikki agrees. "Let's all come!"

"I'll come," Bailey and Elizabeth say at the same time. Bailey laughs, "Jinx!"

"Okay," Bailey nods her head. "As long as we look cute. I haven't asked anyone to the dance. I'm waiting for just the right guy," she smiles. "And I have a feeling I'll find him tonight."

"Okay," I say. "But I'm leaving in… oh my gosh! It's 6:30 already? Okay, I'm leaving soon."

"Soon? Plenty of time to look cute," Bailey says. "Let's go."

We walk until we reach the girls bathroom. Then, we decide to reapply our makeup and brush out our hair again. When we're all finished, we walk out once again. "Ahem," I hear someone cough. "I was wondering if you wanted to dance?"

I turn around to see Brian staring at Nikki. "Um, one sec," White as a ghost, she looks me in my eyes. "What do I do? I've always had a crush on him. Help!"

"Maybe you should dance. It's a risk you should be willing to take," I suggested.

"Yeah," Elizabeth agrees. "Go. Dance. Have fun!"

"Okay," then she turns around to Kaleen, her real BFF. She nods her head. "Okay. I'll do it," she turns to Brian. "Okay. Let's dance," They walk onto the dance floor, gracefully.

"They look really cute together," I acknowledge.

"I know," Kaleen agrees. "I think they're meant for each other."

"Exactly."

"Hey. Wanna dance?" This time, it's Alex. He's staring at Elizabeth.

"Me," Elizabeth asks confused. "Are you talking to me?"

"Yeah."

"Um, sure!"

"Oh, hi Kaleen. Um… would you like to dance?" Nick shows up in a tuxedo.

"Sure," she shrugs. And he leads her onto the dance floor.

"It's not fair!" Bailey whines when they were out of earshot. "I'm the only one here without a boy when I'm the only one who wanted a boy!"

"It's okay," I glance at my phone. "Um, Bailey?"

"Yeah?"

"I have to go."

"But it's only 7:00! Can't you stay later?"

"Yeah, but I'm a little behind in homework. Gosh, I hate history!"

"Fine," she sounded mad.

"Bye! We'll talk Monday," I slowly stand up and walk to the door. "Tell everyone I said goodbye!" I say happily. I walk out and close the door behind me. "Oh, no," I remembered. Matt's Mom was supposed to pick me up! I walked back into the room and once I found Matt (he was sitting next to JJ), I told him, "Matt, you know how your Mom was supposed to pick me up and take me home?"

"Um, yeah," he says.

"Tell her I got a ride," I walk back out and close the door behind me. "Umph," I gasp as a football flies into my stomach making it hard to breathe. "Um," I look up. "Is this yours?"

"Yeah," a tall blond boy with flippy hair answers. "Thanks."

I start to walk away when he says, "Haylie? Haylie Carter?"

"Yeah," I say surprised. "That should be me."

"I heard about you," he tells me. "Guys, come here. Its Haylie Carter!" A bunch of tall, muscled guys about a year older than me, I guessed, came out of the dark night.

"Oh, cool," the tall guy with black hair looks impressed.

"How do you guys know it's——" I was interrupted.

"I used to go to your school."

"Oh," I look confused. "Wait—-Jake?"

"Yep. I thought you would recognize me," Jake was the guy who moved away from Colina some time ago. It was dark, so I didn't recognize him right away.

"So that's Cole, Sean, Michael, Adam… and who's that next to you?"

"Haylie, meet Billie. Billie is my new… middle school friend."

"Oh hi, Billie," I say. "Guys, I'm sorry to say but I have to go now. See you in high school, maybe?"

"Yep. See ya then."

I turn around and walk down a dusty road. Eleven minutes later…

I crack open the door and set down my purse. "Hello," I whisper. "Mom? Is anyone there?" I tiptoe upstairs and into my room. The house looked empty. Deserted. Pitch black. Almost like it was a horror scene in a thriller movie. I was always the person who preferred horror, thriller, or scary movies. Not the heart-warming ones. If I have to watch a romantic movie, it has to have at least some action. I walked across the hall into my parent's room. They were fast asleep. Well, at least my dad was. My mom was reading. "Mom," I whisper. "Hi. When did Dad get home?"

"Oh, about ten minutes ago. The first thing he did was lay down. He skipped dinner because he had a long and hard day at work. Just let him sleep," she says.

"Okay," I said. I was kind of disappointed that I didn't get to see my dad after my first date even though it went terribly.

"Honey," I looked up to see my mother smiling. "How was it?"

"It was…" I moved my position and looked down. "Interesting."

Chapter Eight

"**I**NTERESTING?"

"Interesting," I nodded.

"Great. I'm gonna call Mrs. Grimes and ask her if everything was okay," she put the bookmark in her book and stood up.

"No, Mom!" I jumped up and sat her back down. She gave me a strange look.

"Haylie… what happened?"

"Nothing! Everything's fine, Mom," I tried to convince her. She gave me the same look. The look that says: Haylie, you're crazy. "Fine," I sat down next to her. "It didn't go well," I shifted. "Mrs. Grimes didn't drive me home."

"What? Then who did?"

"No one. I walked."

"Haylie. You know that wasn't the right choice," she took hold of my hands. "You could have called. I would have picked you up!"

"I know. I just wasn't thinking right."

"It's okay, but next time, call me."

"I will."

"Good," she stood up. "Want a cookie?"

"Sure," I took a cookie off of her spotted blue pink and yellow tray. "Yum," I said after taking a bite. "Well, good night!"

"No, Haylie. We're not done here."

"Fine."

"Haylie, you left early. Why?"

"Because I was sick! Yeah…" I coughed and sneezed a few times and held my stomach. "See? Sicker than ever! Well, I better get to bed!" I sneezed again.

"Wait!" She said. "If you're sick, follow me," she stood up and walked over to me. She grabbed my hand and dragged me downstairs and into the kitchen. "So, you're really sick, huh?"

"Yeah…" I coughed. "Super sick… ACHOO!!!" I fake-sneezed. But, if I do say so myself, that was an excellent fake sneeze.

"Whew! Sounds like you're coming down with something! Maybe it's a bad case of the lies," she gave me a look.

"Um," I coughed and looked down. "I've never heard that before. Maybe it's a new disease. I hope they have a cure for it!"

"Really, Hay. What's up?"

"Okay, look," I sat down at the table. She followed me. "He was a jerk Seth told me a story, and I decided he wasn't… nice!" She studied me. "I know, I know. What'd I do wrong?"

"Honey…"

"Wait. Let me guess. 'Don't judge people 'till you know who they really are'?"

"Honey. You're not wrong. It's okay not to like someone. It's not wrong or bad, as long as you have a good reason why," she paused, "Do you?"

"Well, yeah. Matt cheated on Seth's sister!"

"Huh. Well, Haylie. Did it ever come to you that Seth is jealous so he made up a story?"

"No. It was real."

"Haylie," she wasn't convinced.

"Mom. Seth was my crush since I transferred schools to Colina. Plus, he likes me. He wouldn't just lie to me like that," I insisted.

"Well, okay. We should talk tomorrow, though. I'm tired, what about you?"

"Yeah. I'm pretty tired, I guess."

"Well, I'm going to sleep. You don't have to, but keep the noise down, please."

"At 7:30?!" I gasped.

"Yes, Haylie, I'm exhausted!"

"Okay. Good night."

"Love you."

I walked back up to my room and change into my pajama pants and a big shirt. So much for that, since my mom wanted to sleep and everyone else in the house was asleep, I decided it was time. It was texting time. Texting time is usually in the nighttime when no one is awake. It starts when I get a text or I start texting and people join in the little conversation until at least ten people are chatting nonstop. Kaleen, Elizabeth, and I came up with it four months ago. Pretty much anyone who's anyone knows about it.

So I took out my phone from my purse. When I opened it, it said "Four missed calls," I clicked menu, missed calls, and scrolled down. Two of them were from Matt and the other two were from Bailey and Seth. I clicked on Bailey's voice message. It said, "Hey, Haylie! Bailey here. Um, I was wondering where you were on Facebook! Do I sound excited? Yeah? WELL I AM! Ya remember how I was mad that nobody asked me to the dance? Yeah? Well Brendan asked me! Ahhh! Brendan is sooo hot! I'm so excited!!! Okay, I should calm down, now. Another reason I called you was that I was going to ask you if you wanted to do texting time because the 9th person just joined. Well, see ya on the web!"

"Huh," Bailey is WEIRD.

Next… I clicked on Seth's. It said, "Hi, Hay. Well, it's almost 7:15. I was just wondering where ya were and why you disappeared all of the sudden at the dance. Well, call me. I'll answer. Um, okay I gotta go," He sounded disappointed and sad. Poor guy.

I clicked on Matt's message. "Hi. I just wanted to say that I was um, sorry. Um call me back. And maybe we could go to the fall dance together, if you're up for it. Well, call me. I promise I'll answer. Um, bye," Huh. There's no way I'm going on another date with Matt. Not in fall. Not in winter. Not in summer. Not ever.

I then clicked on Matt's second message. "Hello? Haylie? Why aren't ya answering? Hello!? Well, I wanted to tell you in person, but I think, well, I think I like you. Do ya like me? Huh. That was embarrassing, don't ya think? Well, bye!" WEIRD!

I got a call from him again, but ignored it. I checked his voice message. "Hey.

Why'd ya disappear? I was having fun! Weren't you? Well, call me. Bye! Oh, and wait! I almost forgot. I got one more thing. Seth. He's a bad person. Stay away from Seth Stone! Um, well I gotta go. I'm gonna eat now," His message ended. He's telling me to stay away from Seth? Seth told me to stay away from him. "Oh my gosh," I was so CONFUSED! Who is right? Who is wrong? Who should I trust?

This is bad. Really, really bad.

I decided to start texting time. I wanted to know who was in the conversation, first. My buddy list told who was on: Matt, JJ, Billie, Brian, Kaleen, Gwen, Scarlet, Jake, Bailey, Alex, Elizabeth, and Megan, my cousin. I didn't really feel like talking to anyone right now. Sleeping felt like the only thing to do. But then, I decided, I wouldn't be able to think about Matt and Seth. And if I did think about them I wouldn't get to sleep and I would probably be grouchy in the morning.

Five minutes after thinking it through, I decided to sleep so I could eat a good, healthy breakfast in the morning, then think with double the smarts. I turned my phone off and climbed into my twin size pink and black polka-dotted bed. It was hot, so I didn't want covers… I snoozed. (Not snored, snoozed.)

Chapter Nine

I N THE MORNING...

It was 10:37 and I decided it was time to wake up. I crawled out of bed (half asleep). Half way down the stairs (when my eyes were completely open) I noticed a (blurry) strange but somewhat familiar face appeared.

I screamed.

It was Kevin. Kevin. You know, Kev. The one I mentioned at the start of my story. My older brother who I rarely ever see who went off to college.

Well, anyway… where was I? Oh, yeah.

I screamed. "Kevin!!!"

He smiled.

"Kevin! Why are you here? It's not a holiday, is it? Oh, lemme go check my calendar!"

"Haylie."

"No! I should stay and talk to you. No. I'll check my calendar. Or would that be rude?"

"Haylie."

"No I'll stay and chat. Do Mom or Dad know you're here? Or Faith or Sarah or Cole?"

"Haylie!"

"Oh, sorry," I ran and hugged him. "Oh my gosh! Why are you back?"

"Um... here," He reached into his back pocket and pulled out a paper and handed it to me.

I read it through. "What? Why? This is stupid!" The paper said Texas State University was closed for a few months due to technical difficulties and blah blah blah. It was the college he was going to. I looked up at him, teary-eyed. "What does it mean closed? It doesn't mean like, closed, closed... does it?"

"Haylie," he grabbed my hand. "My college closed, my girlfriend just broke up with me, I'm broke since I had to quit my job and I have no place to stay. So the answer to your question is 'yes'."

"Kristy broke up with you?" he nodded. "But, why?"

"She lives in Texas and she refused to have a long distance relationship."

"Did you tell Mom yet?"

"No."

My face grew pale. "What?!"

"I need you to."

"What? No. No way, Kevin."

"Please. I really, really need you to. Oh, please."

"Fine."

"Thanks, but there's also one more thing. Um, I need you to ask her if I can stay over until my college opens again. Or if it doesn't, find a new one, or buy a new house."

"Okay Kevin. But that's it."

"Oh thanks Hay."

"I'm gonna tell her now."

"Wait. Um, I think you should wait until after breakfast. That way, she's in a better mood," he said more smugly than smartly.

"Yes, Oh master. If you're so smart, where are you gonna stay?"

"Um, in your room."

"No! We have a guest room."

"Good."

"When I cough, come out into the kitchen."

"Sounds like a plan," He agreed.

Mom yawned and dragged her lazy self into the kitchen with Dad trailing close behind. "Oh, no! Go, go, go!" I whispered loudly to Kevin as he dashed upstairs into my room. He gently pulled the door shut without a sound.

"Hey, Mom, Dad," I sounded sleepy. I acted sleepy. I was sleepy. That one added to the lie.

"Hi, honey," my dad's voice was scratchy. My mom just nodded.

"Mom. Are you feeling okay? You're usually a morning person."

"I'll be fine… later," she assured me. Knowing what my mom's reply would be like, my dad stated, "I've got a meeting."

"Oh, John. On a Sunday?"

"Yes, I know. I'm sorry. My boss called me an hour ago."

"That early?" My mother's eyes bulged.

"Yes, honey. That early."

"John."

"Honey, it's okay. I won't be home past 5:00. I promise. But I think you should stay in bed."

"I think I might have sore throat."

"Mom, sit down. Dad, you can get ready, I'll take care of Mom."

"Oh, Haylie that would be great!"

"No prob."

Ten minutes later, when the smell of bacon, eggs, and freshly cut fruit was drifting through the house, Kate, Cole, and Sarah walked in a single file and into the kitchen. "I smell bacon!!!" Cole has always loved bacon.

"Sit," I commanded. Their single file broke up and turned into a sloppy triangle with Sarah in front. They took a seat at the table and Mom refused to join them, but to sit alone at the counter. When they pleaded for her to join them at the table, she insisted she was sick and that if she joined the table, they would get her contagious throat sore. They agreed that her idea suited them best.

About halfway through breakfast, I stood up and tapped on my water glass with my fork. "I have an announcement," I looked around to see if I had everyone's attention. I really did. Wow. That actually worked. Huh. I've seen it in movies, but I never actually tried it.

"Um, does everyone kinda remember Kevin, our brother? Cole and Kate and Sarah might not, but Mom does for sure. Well… here," I took out the crumpled paper from my back pocket and handed it to my mom.

"What does it say? Read it, Mommy?" Cole chanted. After reading it, Mom just sat there, speechless. "John!" My dad came in probably in a rush for his meeting. "Oh honey, I really don't have time for… what's this?"

She handed it to him. He just stood there. "Well, where is he?"

"Um, okay let's just say that I talked to him this morning and he said he was broke, homeless, girlfriendless and now he has no schooling," I coughed loudly, causing him to run downstairs and into the kitchen. "Kevin!!!" My mom threw her arms around him. "How did you, but I thought…" she gathered questions like bullets and spit them out at him all at once like a rifle shots.

"You both read it?" Kevin asked in a hushed voice.

They nodded.

Chapter Ten

"Honey," tears in my mom's eyes slid down her face and onto the table "How did you get here?"

"I drove," his eyes moved to Kate, Sarah, and Cole. "Maybe we should sit."

I led them to sit down.

"Haylie?" My mom spoke slowly. "Maybe you should go with the kids upstairs."

"But, Mom!"

"Haylie," My dad's voice strict. "Please go upstairs."

I didn't reply, but I motioned to Cole and he knew it meant to follow me, so he tapped on Kate and motioned upstairs and Kate grabbed Sarah's hand and I led them upstairs. I really wanted to listen to Kevin and my parents, but I knew I had to obey my mom and Dad.

KEVIN AND PARENT'S CONVERSATION:

"Mom, Dad. You read the paper. My college closed. I'm homeless. I was kinda wondering if... well maybe... possibly..."

"Yes?" My dad interrupted.

"Could I crash here for... until I get a home?"

Mom and Dad looked at each other. "Crash?"

"Stay here," Kevin translated.

"Kevin. I guess so. But you sleep in the guest room and you'll be a good brother. No bullying."

"Thanks, Mom!" He got up and hugged her, took one look at my dad's unhappy face they shook hands. "Oh, get over here!" They hugged.

"I'm gonna go tell Haylie!!!"

IN MY ROOM:

Kevin bursts in and tells me he'll be staying. My face glowed with pure excitement. "Kevin, that's great! I—" I was interrupted by my cell phone. It was loud! "I need to take this," I picked it up, changed the volume, and answered the call. "Hello? Haylie here."

"Hi, Haylie. Um are you alone?"

"No I've got my brothers and my sisters and—" I saw my brother pulling Faith out of my room and then he winked at me. I winked back and mouthed the words "Thank you!" to him. "Yeah, I'm alone."

"Good. It's Seth. Um, you know that dance?"

"No. What dance?"

"Um the dance on Monday. It's for school. Are you busy?"

"Um, no, I don't think I am."

"Great! Um wanna go together?"

"Uh… one sec," I covered up the speaker and made sure he didn't hear. Then, I screamed. Very, very loudly, I screamed. "Um, yeah I think I'm free."

"Okay great. Well, it's themed King and Queen Ball. Dress like Queen Elizabeth."

"Okay. I'll call ya later for details."

"Sounds like a plan."

"Cool," We hung up. I felt amazing. Two dates in two days! That's pretty amazing.

Uh oh. If Seth called Brendan will, too. Not good! Beep. My phone alerted me that I had three text messages. The first one was from Megan. It read,

`hey I miss u. tell Kev I luv him 2 'cuz we were just tex-`
`ting and my phone is going dead… would u tell him 4 me?`

```
See u around,

Meggie.
```

That was from my cousin? How did she know Kevin was here? I would have called but her phone is probably dead by now. I texted back,

```
miss u 2 how did u no Kev is here? I didn't know anyone
knew. Who else knows?
```

Send.

While waiting for her to answer back, I read my other text. It read,

```
Hey, babe. It was from my dad. I'm sorry I didn't get 2
say goodbye 2 u 2day was 2 busy 4 me. Halfway 2 work. I'll
see you @ 4:30 or so. I love u!

Daddy.
```

Yes. It's the casual, same old Dad. Must love him!

The next message was from Bailey. It said:

```
Hi Hay Hay Ru coming 2 the dance? If not, lets hang. Call
or text me ill b on my phone whenever u decide to answer
me make sure 2 let me no as soon as possible, ok. I have 2
no so I can decide what I wanna do but it's gonna b based
on ur decision. Answer back soon,

BBailes.
```

I didn't know if I was going to answer her back or not, so I answered my dad back first. I wrote:

```
Hey Daddy it's ok u didn't say goodbye. Ur right, 2day was
definitely tough and busy and hectic 2! Can't wait until
4:30 or so. got something important 2 tell u so don't b
late or else!!! J I'll see u. I luv u!

Haylie.
```

(I always ended my texts with my name.) I was going to tell him and my mom about the date. "See?" I planned to say after I had told him. "Told you it was important."

I decided to text Bailey back.

```
Hey. Haylie here. 'Hay hay?' that brings me back, that
nickname u gave me. Yes, I'm going 2 the dance. Sorry I
couldn't answer sooner; 2day was 2 rough on me. Yes, I am
going 2 the dance… the theme is cool. I guess ill see u
there! Text me,

Haylie.
```

Send.

I needed to ask other people if they were going, too. My text to Elizabeth:

```
Hey it's Haylie I was wondering if u were going 2 the dance
2morrow. Maybe ill see u there? Got a date there with
Seth. Omg I'm sooo exited! Text me back,

Haylie.
```

My text to Kaleen:

```
Hey Ru coming 2 the dance 2morrow? Text me,

Haylie.
```

I started to text to all of my friends. When I finished, I tucked my phone behind my pillow. I sighed. "Hi, guys," No reply. "I know you're there. Come on out, now," I opened my door to see Cole, Sarah, and Faith standing there. And even Kevin! "Oh my gosh," my tan face burned bright red. "Why are you guys listening to me?" I eyed Sarah. "Sarah. Why did you listen to me?"

"Wasn't my idea," she eyed Faith.

"Faith?"

"Not me," she nodded to her left.

"Cole!" I exclaimed.

"Huh?" he acted like this conversation wasn't real. "Oh," He pointed towards Kevin.

"Kevin. Ugh!" I stomped and closed the door.

About five to ten minutes later, I heard a soft voice, "Honey?"

"Whaddya want?"

"Can I come in?" she knocked a couple of times.

"Why?" I asked as if I didn't know.

"We need to talk."

"Right now?"

"Right now," she opened the door slowly and it creaked. "We need to talk," she repeated. "Now," she took a seat next to me. I turned over to face her. "What's wrong?"

"Nothing, Mom."

"Really, hon? What's up?"

"I dunno," I stopped, thinking to myself. "Nothing! I'm fine."

"Honey," she tucked my hair behind my ear. "Are you sure that there's nothing wrong. We could talk. I'll cancel my appointment," she offered.

I gave her a strange look.

"Okay… maybe I'll reschedule it."

That's better. She almost never skipped work. There was one night we had to pry her hands off of her computer to go see Kevin in the hospital when he had a broken leg. "No, Mom. It's fine. I'm fine. I… I guess I'm still a little freaked about Kevin being here. Aren't you?"

She nodded sympathetically. She said goodbye without saying goodbye. I've never liked how my mom works. She wakes up. She makes coffee. She makes calls and takes calls. She types on the computer hour after hour for her boss, who does never understand enough to even give her even one day off! So Sean, her boss, is one of my BIGGEST ENEMIES!!! Sometimes, when I hear how he talks to my mom, I want to yell! Sometimes, I feel like throwing up at the scent of his cologne. Only when I hear, see, or smell him (he wears lots of black cherry scented cologne) do I get this feeling.

So anyway, I decided to lie down and relax when… BEEEP! My phone notifies me that I have one new text message. When I answered it, I saw the text was from Bailey. It read:

so u r going 2 the dance? Cool. The theme is so cool,
right? I can't wait 2 show u my outfit. I know its perfect
4 the dance! So, who r u going with? I'm going alone. But,
only cuz boyz r 2 much 4 me, ya know???
Bailey.

I texted back:

yes u will c me there I do like the theme. I cant wait 4
u 2 show me ur outfit! I am going with Seth. Really? Cuz
boyz r 2 much 4 u? YEAH RIGHT!!!
Haylie.

As far as texting goes, I guess I'm medium speed. Bailey is FAST! If there were a contest for fastest texter alive, she'd win, hands down!!! Most of my friends are pretty quick texters, but not so quick that they're obsessed. (Not counting Bailey. Actually, I don't even know why I still have her number saved in my contacts, and haven't blocked her from texting me, yet!) No. That's only Bailey.

BEEEP! Another text.

BEEEP! Actually two. First one: from Dad. Second one: from Bailey. And…

BEEEP! Okay, third one: from Seth.

This is Dad's text:

```
Hey, babe. What's that somethin' special you want to tell
me about? You know, you could always tell me now. I'm al-
ways all ears when u need me. If u want to save the news
'till I get home, see u then. If not text me 'the important
news', okay? Luv ya, Daddy.
```

My text to him:

```
Heyyy Daddy. I MUST save the 'something special' 'till
when u get home. It's so important, I couldn't POSSIBLY
tell u over texting! I miss u and I'll see u in a few
hours. Luv ya 2,

Haylie.
```

That was pretty much true. It was way too important to tell him over texting or over the phone, so he needed to wait until he got home for the news. He and Mom, that is. I would tell them near dinner's end, when Faith, Sarah and Cole were upstairs getting prepared for bedtime, which was 8:00 sharp, no 'buts', as my mom said.

Anyway, the text from Bailey went like this:

```
Ok ill make sure u get 2 c my outfit 4 the dance, okay? (It
is too because I cant stand boyz!!! LOL we both no that's
a lie!!!) Text me,

Bailey.
```

Yes. It's typical, average Bailey.

```
okay. See u 2night.

Haylie.
```

I answered Seth's text next. He wrote:

```
hey. So I guess ill c u at the dance, right? Got a good
costume? I don't. Going shopping right now. I don't know
how girls do it. I'm dieing of boredom after less than one
hour of shopping. HOW DO U DO IT?
```

Oh, Seth. How cute can he get? V-E-R-Y! Then I texted him:

```
C me at the dance? Yes you will I do not have a good cos-
tume, but ill make due. U DON'T KNOW HOW GIRLS DO IT???
Not all girls are shoppoholics. I'm not. I get bored after
30 MINUTES OF SHOPPING!!! C u at the dance…

Haylie.
```

Although it wasn't completely and totally true that I got bored after 30 minutes of shopping (maybe an hour) I had to make him feel better somehow, right?

Then, it happened. Yes, it. Someone rang the doorbell.

Okay. I know it sounds like it's not a big whoop, but if you knew who it was then you would be excited too.

Anyway, I jumped off of my bed and dashed downstairs to see who it was. I saw my mom rubbing her eyes and yawning halfway to the door and Sarah and Kevin arm in arm coming downstairs all heading for the door.

Kevin answered the door, "Ohhh, it's only Kaleen," He grunted.

"Shut up, Kevin."

"You shut up!"

I grunted. "Just… leave…"

"Kevin. That's quite enough, now. Now I'll go back to bed. Haylie, invite Kaleen in, and Kevin I'd like you to drive the kids to the market and pick up some things. I've got a list for you in the kitchen. And, please! Take as long as you'd like. Maybe, if they are good, you can take the kids out for i-c-e-c-r-e-a-m," she spelled it out so the kids couldn't understand that she was really saying ice cream.

"Hey! Mom, are you being a show-off?"

"What, honey?"

"A show-off. You're showing-off that you can spell big words!"

"Honey, I wasn't being a show-off."

I gave Kevin a little look that I like to call, ha.

She sighed and muttered something under her breath, which sounded like, "And, whatever anyone does, remember: I'M TAKING A NAP!"

"Okay," I paused before saying, "Come in," and closing the door after her.

She nodded a polite nod. "So. Do you have your costume yet?"

"I might," I looked just about as unsure as I was. "In the basement——Mom? We'll be in the basement looking for a costume——we have a bunch of things from when my mom and Dad were a kid."

"Whoa, Haylie. You're parents aren't that old, are they?" she said when she saw the long elegant dresses and puffy pants.

"Well, no. That's not the point."

"Then what is?" she questioned, looking confused.

"Well, I also have clothes from when their parents were kids. And their parents and their parents, and I think they are old enough, but not too old that their clothes won't fit me."

There was a ladder into my basement. But it wasn't like spooky and freaky and had lots of spiders. There were plenty of windows, which made it bright. I liked it there. It always felt cozy to me. In fact, I wouldn't mind sleeping in there for a night or two.

Next, I opened the latch (with a little bit of Kaleen's help) and invited her down first.

She shrugged, took the ladder in her hands, and started making her way down.

"Watch out for the stool!" I warned her. Everyone trips on the stool. There was a stool at the end of the ladder. I put it there so that I wouldn't have to jump. (When I was a kid and I would have to jump halfway down the ladder just to get down.) She carefully stepped onto the stool before she sat down in my brother Kevin's old favorite chair. He never let anyone but himself sit on it. I was about to say something, but I didn't feel like it. Then, I decided that that decision was by far the best of the day.

I climbed down the ladder pleased with myself, and immediately started digging through the big bin with hundreds of (they looked like costumes) clothes from my past relatives. "Hey!" I exclaimed while pulling out a golden dress. It was beautiful. "Should I try it on? Or should I wait until I find some other dresses and try them on at the same time?"

"Definitely you should wait until you find more," she told me.

"Okay," I set the dress on the trunk next to it, which had toys from my mom and Dad's childhood. Or did it have wedding pictures? I don't know.

Then, I kept on looking and then paused. "Do you have your costume yet?"

"Me?" she sat up straight. "No, not yet. Why?"

"If you want, you can look through the next bin to my left. On my right, it's either pictures of the wedding or toys of my mom and Dad's, so you probably don't want to go in there."

"Oh," she sat up a little bit more straight. "Okay," she stood up and walked to my left, gave me a friendly smile, and then went to work right away. "Hey!" She said almost right away. "Look. This is nice. I like it."

"Yeah, me too," she had pulled out a blue dress with golden designs going down the sides. Honestly, I did like it. These clothes weren't too bad.

About a half an hour later I had seven dresses and she had nine. "Good. I think we pretty much went through everything. Wanna try things on, now?"

"Yeah," she nodded in agreement.

"Okay," I decided. "I'll go into the bathroom next to the closet near the hall. You stay in here, okay? When I come down, we'll show each other's outfit and decided which one is the best together."

"'Kay. Bye for now."

I waved before going out of the basement and into the bathroom.

About half an hour later, we were both finished. She went first to get her dress picked.

"I like dress C best. What about you?" I asked.

"No, I liked A. It suits my skin tone better," she laughed.

"Hey, looks like the judges have a draw!" I said in my best announcer voice. "Hey! Let's ask my mom! Do you want to?"

"Sure. Let's go," she agreed.

"I'm sure she's not asleep," I assured her when he asked about it. "She's probably better."

Sure enough, when I knocked on her door, she said, "Come in," she didn't sound excited, but she didn't sound asleep.

I opened the door. "Hi, Mom." When I saw what she was fully occupied doing, I grunted and groaned. "MOM!"

"Yes, honey?" her head didn't turn away from the computer screen. She was FULLY occupied WORKING! Ugh. And, have I mentioned, I HATE her boss. I know I already mentioned that, but it's VERY true. And people say hate is a strong word.

That's why I use it.

"Mom," I decided to try to calm down, because Kaleen was there. "I know you're busy, but this will only take a second," I led Kaleen into her room. "Okay. Which dress do you like best? This one?" I held up the one Kaleen liked. "Or this one?"

I gave her a minute to decide. "Well, they're both very nice."

"Mom. Seriously," My face turned from a smile to a blank, serious expression, so she knew I wanted serious.

"Hmmm. Honestly, I don't know."

"Mom! Choose."

"Okay! Um, I think I like the one on the left. There. Can I work, now?"

I nodded and was shocked. KALEEN had defeated me!

She had picked the one Kaleen liked!

"I told you! The one I liked was better!" she squealed.

"I guess you're right," I gave in.

"Okay, let's do yours now," she suggested.

"Let's go," We were halfway to the basement when the door creaked open. First, I saw Cole come in, followed by Kate and Sarah and Kevin. I gasped. "Come on!" I ran to the latch to the basement. I didn't want for Kevin to be bugging us. As quietly as I possibly could, I opened the latch and let her in first. What? That was good manners!

Once we were both in, I held up all of the dresses I liked. There were seven. One was gold with sparkles on the torso and halfway down the dress. The rest of the dress faded into a fainter gold, almost like a golden yellow. The next one was rosy pink and the top half was glittery and the rest was pretty nice. Then, there was a beautiful golden colored dress that reached the floor, no problem! It was beautiful, but a little too fancy for me, so I threw it out of the pile and put it into the bin where it came from. There was this elegant white dress that barely touched the floor, but I decided to wear it for when I actually got married. I handed it to Kaleen and she put in the bin where it came from. I also picked a pink dress that wasn't too long and had a black middle. That was one of my favorites. Then I had a pink dress that had ruffles form the torso down. I liked that one. I also liked one with a blue color. It was strapless. That was the last one.

About fifteen minutes later, we decided to pick the one with a strapless top which was blue. She liked the one with pink ruffles and sparkles. This time, we did eenie meenie minie mo. And who do you think won? ME! This, I was happy about.

Then she announced, "Well, I've got to get home. I'll see you at the dance, okay?"

"Okay. See you then!"

"Wait! So, are you going with Seth?"

"Yeah, he asked me Monday after school," I said.

"So, your Mom's totally chill about it?"

"Yeah, she really doesn't care. It's my dad I'm worried about. But, I asked my mom to talk him about it, anyway. No way he'll say no, he always listens to my mom."

"Good."

(Awkward silence.)

"So are you going with anyone?" I asked.

"No, but I'm hoping you know who will be there."

"Ohh!" I squeal.

"Hey! I don't 'ohh!' when you talk about Seth!"

"Fine, sorry."

"So, see you there, then?"

"Yes you will. And, good luck with——"

"Shhh!"

"I was going to say you know who!" I said.

See, Kaleen doesn't like talking about crushes… well… anywhere, really. I have to respect that, as she is my best friend.

"Bye!"

She climbed up the ladder and closed the front door behind her.

I remained in the basement.

Why, you ask?

To think.

To think about Seth. To think about friends. To think about how much fun the dance was going to be.

And I did.

Chapter Eleven

"**H**AYLIE! PHONE!" MY MOM YELLED in a scratchy tone. Once I entered the kitchen, I told her to stop shouting or she'd lose her voice permanently. At that, she scurried off into her bedroom and closed the door. I made and assumption that she was typing on her computer. Working, no doubt. I took the phone she had set on the counter. "Hello? Who is this?" I asked into the phone.

"Haylie? Hi. It's Elizabeth. You're on speaker with me and Kaleen and Nikki."

"Oh," I said as I traveled into the living room where it was quieter. "Hi."

"We've been calling you for half an hour! What have you been doing?"

"Well, after Kaleen came over to find an outfit for the dance, I kind of stayed in my basement and got tired… I'm really sorry, but I think I fell asleep."

"Right… so you're going to the dance, then?" she assumed. Before I had a chance to answer, she said, "Do you have a costume yet? I do."

Nikki added, "Me too! I found one at Nordstrom and got accessories at Claire's. They have the BEST accessories! My dress is black and has rips and tears. It's perfect for me! Of course, the price was a little high and the rips are supposed to be there. People keep asking about the rips. It's annoying when I have to tell them that they're supposed to be there. Then again, Elizabeth thinks my dress looks pretty comical. I almost killed her when she said pretty, and I didn't know she was going to say pretty comical. Well, I didn't strangle her. Or else she'd be dead. Which she isn't… she's here right now. Say 'hi', Elizabeth! Wait, no. Let me say hi for you. Elizabeth says 'hi'. Are you excited for the dance? I am. Well, kind of. I've never been the happy or excited type, but this seems fun. I know, I know, I never say 'fun', but… it does seem pretty cool. I heard you were going with Seth. Is that true, or us it just a rumor? Well, people say it's true, but you can never believe roomers unless you hear the truth from the actual person. Which is true, but I thought, you know, since you guys are so perfect for each other and stuff… I thought it was true. Is it? Wait, let me guess! Yes! It's true, isn't it? I know it is, don't lie. So… you excited?"

That was so fast; I swear it sounded like a mouse yap, yap, yapping away… in dog language, or something. I was shocked; I didn't know she could talk like that. Or talk at all! She barely ever talked. BARELY. You probably don't believe me, thought, considering how much she just talked. It probably made up for the rest of her soundless life. Elizabeth is the girly-girl. Kaleen and I are just… sort of in the middle.

"Um, yeah. I guess… I'm excited…" I say, sounding a little bit unsure, which I totally was. I couldn't hear what she was saying because it was SO FAST!!!

"Can I come with you on the way back? My mom already said she'd take me there, but it's going to be too late for her to pick me up," Kaleen said.

"Well, I'm going with Seth. So, no," I glanced over. The clock in the living room said it was almost 5:00! I wasn't going to be ready by then unless I was set for light speed! And, I know two hours sounds like lots of time, but it's really not. Well, at least it's not for me. I have to curl my hair, do my makeup, brush my teeth, put on my dress, eat, check and double check everything, add extra accessories, and triple check everything.

And, I'm not even sure that's all I have to do! Who knows: my mom could throw in a random chore, or something. Deciding it was time to hang up, I said, "Well, I have to get ready. Seth's gonna pick me up at seven and I don't have a lot of time to get ready, so I have to go."

"Okay, I'll see you at the dance!" Elizabeth replied. "Bye!" Nikki said. There was no reply from Kaleen, though. I waited to hear something come from her mouth. I waited and waited, until I heard the dial tone. I dragged my body weight into the kitchen and hung up the phone on its charger before dashing upstairs and into my room.

Then, I remembered that I had left my dress downstairs in the basement. I groaned before running back downstairs. Kevin, Cole, and my dad were standing there.

"Dad! I didn't know you were home!" I said.

"I just got home about five minutes ago," He told me. When I got a better look at what they were all doing, I asked, "What's this?"

"Oh, nothing. Just… nothing," Kevin choked out.

"Uh huh…" I looked suspicious. "Really? SO you're telling me that you are all here, and Dad is home for… nothing?" I thought about Nancy Drew. She always said that you should look for the weakest suspect. Cole wasn't a suspect, but the situations were somewhat related. And, technically, he was the weakest.

"Cole," I narrowed my eyes at him. "If you don't tell me, I'll tell Mom that you were the one who took the last gingersnap," I warned.

"He doesn't care! Do whatever you want! He's not gonna break!" Kevin warned back at me.

"Now, guys. Let's be fair. I think Haylie has every right to know," my dad stood up for me.

"No, she doesn't! She has no rights! This plan is working against her knowledge!!!"

"Kevin…" Dad warned.

"But——"

"No 'buts'. Haylie is going to find out sooner or later, so it's better to tell her sooner, don't you think?"

"Fine, Dad," Cole said, trying not to get on Dad's bad side.

"Whatever," Kevin didn't sound convinced but agreed anyway.

"Thanks, Dad," I mouthed to him.

He smiled back. Before speaking…

Then he said out loud, "Haylie, there's nothing to show, but there is something to say."

When he stopped and looked at me, I had to say, "And that is…?"

"Well, the boys of the family are thinking that they aren't being treated very well," He explained slowly.

"Yeah! Girls should get chores, too! It's not fair how we get all of the chores around here!" Cole yelled. We all stared at him in astonishment. He has always been a great little kid. As a baby, he met every standard he needed to be a regular baby much faster than average babies take. As a kid, he made new friends, and was now achieving high grades in all subjects and always has A's and B's, doing very well in school.

So… what had just happened???

"Well," my dad said slowly. "The boys—and just the boys—are planning to play a trick on all of the girls. Maybe a random pillow fight. Or, maybe an unexpected water balloon fight would be good. Don't think of it as revenge think of it as a little fun to cheer everyone up. After that, we might explain how we feel… and then throw some more unexpected water balloons."

"Oh. Okay… So that's it?"

"Yeah. That's all we were doing," Kevin answered. "And now we have nothing to do since you know. Way to go, Haylie. You screwed up an entire afternoon. Good thing you'll be gone on a date later!" He smirked.

"Hey! How did you…? I'M GONNA KILL YOU!" I screamed.

"Honey, what date? Why didn't you tell me about a date?"

"Well, I was going to tell you. That was the really important thing I just had to tell you about, in person."

"Well, now! I vote to talk now!"

"Dad…" I said.

"No! I'm not busy! You don't look busy. Let's talk right now!"

"Actually, I am busy. I've got to get ready for the dance. Well, I was going to tell you, but since you already know, there's no reason to talk! Well, I'm gonna go get ready. Bye!" I said quickly before dashing to the basement. Then, I open the latch and climbed in, snatched the dress. After that, I climbed right back up the ladder. Yes, I thought to myself. I got it!

When I had the dress, and had already snuck by Dad, Cole, and Kevin, I trotted into my room. I applied my makeup in less than forty-five minutes. (It would have taken less, but Cole came in and it took me a long time to get him out.)

Next, I took my dress and, before trying it on, checked the clock. 6:02! I would not be ready on time. Running, panting, and on the verge of sweating, I finally had the dress and makeup on and iron plugged in. I brushed through my hair and was half finished with curling it, when… ding-dong! The doorbell rang. I checked the clock. 6:24, it wasn't time, yet! I wanted to see who it was, anyway, so I ran downstairs.

"Hello," a pretty girl said. She looked to be about eighteen. "Is Kevin here?"

"Um, yeah. May I ask who this is?" I said. I really had no idea, but she did seem familiar. Very familiar.

"Oh. Sorry. Well, I'm Kristy, Kevin's old girlfriend. See, we broke up when the college closed, because of what our distance would be, if we were still together. My mom surprised me when she said that we were moving to California. So… here I am!"

"Oh. Just one second. Come in." I led her into the living room and she sat down on a couch, admiring the house.

"Kevin! Kevin, come quick!" I ran upstairs and knocked on the door, decided to barge in… and then barged in. "Kevin. You'll never believe… Kristy's here! She moved to… here! To California! She's living here!"

He gasped. "No. I don't believe you," he said while lifting weights. He was obviously working out.

"If you don't believe me, come see!" He didn't budge. "Come on!" I grabbed his hand, and pulled him downstairs.

When he saw her he gasped. "Kristy! It's you!" he ran and hugged her. He whispered something in her ear and came over to me. "Haylie. I need a huge favor," he said slowly.

"Wait," I said. "Rewind and pause," then, I paced into the kitchen and picked up the phone. "Hey," I said when Seth answered. "It's me, Haylie. I was actually kind of wondering if you could pick me up around 7:30. Would that be okay?"

"YES! It would be great! My mom is freaking out and doing my hair all fancy-like. I don't think I'll be ready by 7:00 either. Well, bye!" He hung up. I walked back into the living room. "Okay. Go for it," I said to Kevin.

"Well, Kristy offered to take me out on a dinner date tonight, and… well, I know you have something planned, but… I'm gonna need you to watch the kids."

For a minute, I just stood there, in too much shock to speak. I had always been a nice girl, always doing things for other people. But this… this was different! Seth and I had never been on a date together! I couldn't just say no… could I? I mean, maybe I could, but then I'd be too mean, and people would never even talk to me! People would think I was a total jerk! I didn't want that to happen.

"What? No, I can't. I just…" I sat on the couch and fluffed my hair. "I just can't! Seth asked me to… well, I mean, I could, but if I can, then can't you?"

"No," He starts to walk over to Kristy. He sat down next to her. "No, Kristy and I are going out, tonight. I'm busy."

"NO! I'm busy! I never have a day to myself! Its… it's not fair!" I walked right over to him.

"Now, hold on. What's going on here?" My mom and Dad both entered the room. My mom looked mostly better, as if she'd never gotten sick at all. Almost. "Why are you constantly fighting?"

"Mom! He wants me to watch the kids! I actually have plans!" I tried to defend myself.

"Dad! Kristy just got here and we want to go out tonight! I don't wanna watch them!" he yelled. Actually, it was like good old times, when we used to fight: when 'the kids' never even existed.

"Oh, hi, Kristy! I'm really sorry. Why don't you go up to Kevin's room? Or you could introduce yourself to the kids!" My mom offered.

"Mom!" Kevin screamed.

"Now calm down. Since your mother is recovering, she may be able to watch one kid," My dad assured us.

"Yeah," I said. "One kid. What about the other two?"

"You will both take one kid with you to wherever you're going," He told us in a stern voice.

"That's not FAIR!" Kevin yelled. "No!"

"Fine. Then, you're both going nowhere. Case closed," he said. He seemed annoyed. I wasn't trying to be annoying.

"Whatever, I'll take one," I finally gave in.

"Good. Kevin, so will you. Kate! Cole! Sarah!" He turned his attention to the staircase. "Come down here, now."

"No!" Kevin complained and denied. "Why can't YOU?!"

"Because."

"Because!!!!!! Because why!!!!!"

My dad simply ignored him.

When Kate, Sarah, and Cole came down, my dad told them, "Haylie will be taking one of you to a dance, and Kevin will be taking one of you on a date."

"What about the third one?" Kate asked, confused. "Where will the third one go?"

"Well," my dad answered. "One will stay with Mommy."

"Okay," Kate said. She seemed to be satisfied. "One two three, I call Haylie!"

"No! That's no fair!" Cole yelled. "I call Haylie!"

"No, I call her!" Sarah argued. "That's no fair! I want her!"

My dad left the room saying, "Settle this alone, okay?"

"Fine," I said. Then, I turned to them. "Stop," I picked up Kate and held Sarah's hand. Cole nudged her and tried to get my hand.

"Will you stop?" I wasn't just talking to Cole. They were all being aggressive. "Well, letting them pick is not going to work, obviously. We need to find another plan. Like a... like a plan B. We need a plan B," I reported.

"No duh," Kevin snorted.

"Okay. What if they pick. Like from a hat or something. That would be fair enough, right?"

"Yeah!" Cole agreed.

"I'll be back!" I jogged upstairs. In my drawer, there were hats... and lots of them. I picked one: the one that was plain and black. I liked that hat, but I figured that I could spare it just for this situation. I picked another: just plain white. I brought them into the kitchen and ripped three pieces of paper; writing mine, Kevin's, Mom's, Kate's, Cole's, and Sarah's names. I placed Cole's, Sarah's and Kate's name in the black one and Kevin's, Mom's, and my name in the white one.

"Okay! I've got it. So each child will pick a name out of each hat. It will determine who they will go with. Kate. You can go first, then Sarah. Not Cole because there will only be one person left, so Cole will be with the person who is basically stuck with the last one," I said, taking a long breath afterwards.

Kate walked up to me and picked one name out of each hat. "Hey! I picked Sarah and Kate and Haylie! We can both come with you! Yes!" Kate said in exclamation.

"Oh, no. Kate. Only pick two, please," I said. "And, this time... DON'T open your eyes, okay?"

"Fine," she put them back and picked two more. She read them aloud, "I got Cole and Mom," she told us.

"Okay. Cole, you'll be staying with Mom. Now you can pick, Sarah," I said in an official voice.

"Okay," she walked over to me when Kate sat down. I could tell that he was disappointed, but this was the only fair way... that I could think of, anyway. "I got…" she dug into the hats, which, compared to her, looked pretty huge. "Kevin and Kate! That means I'm gonna go with Haylie!" She squealed

"Yes, it does. Well, there you have it," I told Kevin. "You'll take Kate, I'll take Sarah, and Cole stays home."

Cole buried his face in a pillow and cried. HE CRIED! Now, I felt bad. "Cole? What's wrong?" Even thought I knew, I had to ask. That was like… the official thing to say when someone is sad, or when they get hurt. No, it is not a written rule, but everyone knows it's official.

"Well, I have to stay here alone, and I wanna GO SOMEWHERE!" He screamed.

"Shhh, Cole. Stop yelling," I walked over to him, picked him up, and sat down on the couch. I set him on my lap. "Who do you want to go with?"

"YOU!" He kept crying.

"Shhh, Cole! Be quiet or we'll get in trouble!" When I said it, he stopped, almost suddenly. "You can go with me, then! Do you want to?" By trying to make things better, I made them much worse.

"Okay," He got up and wiped his tears.

"Hey! Why does he get to come with you, and I don't? It's just not fair!" Kate yelled.

"Fine, fine, fine! Everyone just, please stop yelling!" I said. Really, I didn't want them to come, but it was clear, I had to let them. If I had said no, they'd tell Mom and she'd make me take them all. It was better just to give in now, I figured.

"Kevin, I'm taking all of them, so I'm gonna need you to get them ready. Something fancy would be great. Tell me when they're all ready," I ran back upstairs and finished to other half of my hair. After about twenty minutes, there was a knock at the door. This time, I knew, it was definitely Seth.

"Me! It's for me! Kevin? Do you have the kids ready? We need to go, now! Please hurry," I shouted all at once while running down the stairs. "Hurry! He's here," I warned myself when I continued down the stairs. "Hi! Come in," I said after I had opened the door.

"No, I can't. My mom is waiting outside. Are you ready to go, now?" he says.

"Yeah… but here's the thing. So, Kevin… I mean… well I need to watch my siblings tonight," I said fast instead of slow because I needed to get it out of the way… and fast!

"Oh. Well then maybe we can go out another night?" he said in a voice that told me he was upset... very upset.

"No. That's not what I meant. I can still come," Although I could see how he thought that I couldn't come, I had to tell him, anyway. "But, I have to bring my sisters and brother. Is that okay?"

"Um... I don't know. Is it something you have to do or something you want to do?" It didn't seem like he loved the thought of it not being just us. (Well, just us... and the whole school, that is.) Why did I ever agree to take Cole too? Why did I ever agree to take any of them? These were the questions I started asking myself.

"Something I have to do. My parents told Kevin and me to take one of them. We each picked a Kate and Sarah. Cole was sad that he wasn't picked and because he had to stay with Mom. Seth, it's definitely something I have to do," Assuring him, I grabbed his hand and pulled him in the house. "COLE! SARAH! KATE! Are you ready? We're leaving right now," As I was saying it, they all rushed to the door. "Thank you! Now come on!" We went outside. Lucky for us, Seth's Mom's car was a decent, and we could all fit in it all right. One problem solved before it even was a problem! Off to a good start, I guess.

So Seth sat in the front, Cole, Sarah and Kate sat in the middle and I sat in the back.

None of us started talking until I started to make conversation.

Chapter Twelve

"So," I said, "WHAT ARE we gonna do at the dance?" I almost exclaimed but I realized that I really wasn't happy. The kids were coming. And, I know that if I said that statement out loud (the kids were coming) "the kids" would get mad! I dared not take the risk.

"I dunno. Dance. Eat," Cole also sounded extremely bored. "Things I do on a regular day basis."

Laughing, I asked, "Are you bored? Sick, maybe? What's wrong, Cole? You don't sound too excited but before we left the house, you were really happy. What's up?"

"No. I'm fine. I… ACHOO! I'm fine. Really," He didn't sound fine. We sounded more like he was… sick!

"You're sick aren't you? Can I drop you off with Kevin or take you home?" This was it: my excuse to drop one kid. Now, all I need is two more excuses! This didn't sound too bad, after all.

"No! I'm fine——ACHOO!!! I'm fine, trust me… ACHOO!!!" I could tell that he really wanted to come with us. I didn't blame him: he liked being with the "big kids," and claimed he was one.

"Okay. Tell me if you need anything; don't wander off by yourselves, and-most importantly: stay with me. If you aren't with me, then at least stay with each other. If you don't listen, of course, there will be consequences, and that's a promise!" I told them, sternly. I wasn't too good at being stern, so it came out choppy. I knew they could tell what I had meant.

But, the bad thing about rules and disciplining them was realizing that I was turning into my mother!

I tried to shield the thought.

"Okay! We get it," Sarah told me.

"Yeah. We'll listen, don't worry about us," Kate said intelligently. "We're civilized people."

While I laughed, I said, "Okay, just make sure you follow the rules, guys," I warned them.

In-between words, Cole was coughing and sneezing.

"Cole! You sure you don't wanna go home or something? I… think you're really sick! It might not be smart to go inside the dance."

"Well… I dunno. I feel kind of sick, I admit it. I don't wanna go, though," He replied.

Mrs. Stone interrupted us, "We're here! Haylie, honey? Would you like some help out? Seth! Help Haylie out. Oh, Haylie! You look adorable! I need a picture. Seth? Strike a pose, now!"

Mrs. Stone demonstrated a few poses. Seth shielded his eyes, and shook his head. "Mom…"

"It's okay, Seth," I laughed.

I replied to Mrs. Stone's questions, "No, Mrs. Stone. I don't need help out. Picture? Sure. Seth, it's okay. I don't mind, do you?" Answering all of her questions in one breath, I inhaled and exhaled again. Wow. Inhaling and exhaling really do work. I did NOT know that. I tried it a couple of times. We posed for pictures: two of only Seth and me, and two more of everyone in the car. I even took one of Seth and his mother… that one was really nice.

"Okay, Mom. Enough pictures, now. We have to go inside. We're already late as it is," Seth warned his mother, struggling out of her grip. She had been hugging him for the whole time he'd been talking.

"Oh, I love you, Seth. Have a good time Haylie! Are you positive you don't want me to take the kids back to my house? I'm sure they'd like that! I bought lots of board games about two days ago, so we could play," she offered.

"Oh, that would be perfect! Thank you," I turned my attention to Kate, Sarah, and Cole. "Do you want to go to Mrs. Stone's house? It would be great fun!"

"Should uh, I dunno. I will if they do..." Sarah questioned.

"Yes! Please go. It will be more fun for you guys," I added, mumbling.

Seth laughed. "Yeah. Go on, guys."

"Why?" Cole asked.

"Well," Seth answered, "because if you do, I'll let you play with my old action figures! In fact, you can have them!"

Cole gasped. "Really? Thanks!"

"Ha! Not feeling so sick anymore, Cole?" Mrs. Stone implied.

"I... eh hem! Yeah, I'm..." he fake sneezed.

Everyone turned to him.

"What?" Cole asked.

No one said anything.

"What about me?" Kate asked. "Me and Sarah?"

"Sarah and me," I corrected her.

"Okay, Sarah and me," she gave in. "What about Sarah and me?"

"Well, my little sister, Rosie is home. You can play with her. She's got a lot of dolls. Do you like dolls?" Seth tried.

"Yeah," Kate and Sarah answered together. They looked at each other. "Jinx!" Kate yelled. "Ha! Can't talk until I say your name, Sarah!"

"You just did," she smirked.

"Darn!" Kate paused, and continued, "We both like dolls. In fact, if you add up both of our doll collections together, we have over fifty!" Exclaiming, she spread her arms both ways in a stretch. "I can line them up like this!"

Seth smiled, "Cool!" He grinned and we glanced at each other. "Okay, Mom. They're coming with you. Love you!" He hugged his Mom one more time and walked back over to me. "Bye," Every one of us waved to each other as we were walking into the gymnasium. This was our school. I knew how its layout was by now. It was pretty big, for a middle school... or at least that's what I thought when I first came to the school. I'm going to tell you about my very first day at this school. Here's how I remember it:

When I walked onto the school property, the principle greeted me kindly. "Hello," I remembered he had said to me. "This is Colina. I'm sure you'll find this school appropriate for you. It has been the middle school for many Harvard students. As I remember it, your principle told me that you were a very bright student."

(I blushed at that!)

"I hope you will like the students here. Most are very kind; however, every school has their bullies. Of course, I do try to stop them before they do anything inappropriate," He walked me to my classroom. When we were halfway there, he said to me, "You've been far too quiet. Is everything okay? Do you need anything?"

"No. I'm fine, thank you. I'm just as nervous as any other kid would be on their first day. Thank you for walking me to my classroom. I can walk there from here."

"Okay, Hayden. Thank you for choosing Colina middle school. The teacher will ask one of the students if they would give you a tour. I'm sure there will be many offers for such a wonderful girl," He had said.

I remember I had started laughing. He had called me Hayden! Hayden! I remember Seth, Michelle, Elizabeth, Brendan, Kaleen, and Nikki offering to give me a tour. Mrs. Bartelstone had picked Kaleen. All I remember was that by the end of the tour, I really liked the school. I made lots of friends quickly, too.

I had met Seth, and realized he was very friendly and nice to me.

By the time I was done with thinking up that flashback, we were already in the gym.

"This is it," I said, and squeezed my arm, trying to look casual. "I'm here."

This was make it or break it, right here. Could I walk in heels?

Could I keep it up for the hours we would be here?

Would I fall face first?

Make it or break it.

Chapter Thirteen

"**H**EY! WHERE HAVE YOU BEEN?" Alex asked me. Weird. He always came off to me as just plain weird. It seems to me that he's at every dance I've been to and he is always the first one to greet me. He's actually, really nice. Elizabeth really likes him. And, I think he really like her.

I think.

"Oh, uh sorry," I wasn't really paying attention to his question, (because I was thinking) but I remembered it quickly. "I just came late, I guess."

"Oh. Cool," he said. We kind of just stood there for a minute. "Did you hear there's a chocolate fountain? It's pretty cool. They have strawberries, and the chocolate is hot so you can make strawberry s'mores!"

"Oh. That's cool. I'll definitely look into that. Thanks. Well, I'd better go now."

He bit into a taco in response.

Okay. I guess that meant goodbye. Really, I had no clue. All he ever did was eat, basically.

I'm not saying he was fat.

He wasn't.

He just seemed to eat every time I saw him.

"Um, okay…" I said to myself as I walked away with Seth.

"So, how have you liked Colina so far?" Seth asks.

"Well, it's pretty good. So far, I've met lots of people, all very nice."

I really didn't want to say anything else, because the year wasn't over, yet. I had to say, "so far," for that reason. I walked over to a vacant bowl of punch. Pouring myself a glass, I said again, "So far…" Just to make sure he knew…

"Well, good. We'll try to keep it that way," Seth said.

Nodding, I started to walk even more into the gymnasium, seeing Nikki and Kaleen and Elizabeth.

"Ahhh! You're here!" Elizabeth squealed.

Her dress was purple with cute mini ribbons scattered all over her dress. It was really pretty, in my opinion.

Nikki's was black and shredded and ripped, like she said. I do have to admit. It was very nice.

Since Kaleen was over at my house and I gave her the dress she was wearing, you already know how her dress is.

"Yay," Nikki didn't sound as amused as Elizabeth.

"Did you see the chocolate fountain? It's amazing," said Kaleen holding a half-eaten chocolate-covered strawberry. "AMAZING!" She repeated.

"Actually, no, I have not tried the chocolate fountain because I just got here!" I exhaled one more long breath (trying to look casual again) and looked at Seth. "Elizabeth, Kaleen, Nikki. You guys know Seth."

"Yeah. Hey," as always, Nikki being her old self: excited and happy! Just kidding. I just described Elizabeth, her COMPLETE opposite.

"Hi," Seth responds, smiling. "I've seen you around campus. Nikki, right?"

"Nikki. Right," still, she sounds even plainer then before.

"And I'm Elizabeth! It's nice to meet you! Well, we've already met, but we haven't totally formally met yet. And now we are, so… good! Nice to meet you… again!" Elizabeth says with ten times the enthusiasm as Nikki would EVER say a single word with… unless being sarcastic, of course.

And when we were on the phone… what was that about? She said she was excited… but… WOW. Guess she doesn't really talk in public.

"Wow! You're just really excited, aren't you?" Seth couldn't think of anything else to say, I could tell.

"Yup! Big ball of energy is what people call me... He, I like that! Just start calling me Elizabeth Big Ball of Energy Campbell!"

"Oh. Okay..." He paused. "So then you're Kaleen..." He leans over to shake her hand.

"Yeah. That's me!" With all her strength, she turned Seth's hand counterclockwise. "Ha! Does that hurt?" she said, letting go of his hand.

"Nice to meet you too...?" Seth said stifling back.

"Oh sorry," Seth was surprised when she burst into a laugh. "Really, Seth. I was only joking. I'm not tough! I'm as strong as a mouse!" She WOULD NOT stop giggling hysterically.

"Well, you seemed pretty strong when you twisted my arm around 360 degrees!" he said, not convinced.

"No. I'm not. You only thought I was strong because you wanted to. Well, at least that's what I read in this new book I bought from the bookstore in Simi Valley! You should read it!"

"Gee, thanks. I dunno if would really be into that, but..." he said.

"You don't know that you don't like it until you try reading it! Try it, you'll like it, trust me."

"Um, okay. I guess I'll look into it..." He muttered, still rubbing his hand.

"You'll love it!" She paused. "Hey! Why don't you say hello to Alex? Nikki said, "Hey... if you do, Elizabeth can come! Oooo Elizabeth's got a crush."

Elizabeth blushed. "No!" She blushed again. "Okay, maybe a little bit!"

"Oooo!" Kaleen said.

"Oooo. Elizabeth's got a crush. I'm gonna go check out the snack table," Nikki said. She just walked away. Just like that. NO enthusiasm whatsoever. I was pretty sure that we were all thinking the same thing: She's weird!!! I guess she's simply Goth in public.

"So, Elizabeth. Want to see how Alex is? Kaleen, you can come to," I volunteered to cut the silence.

"Um... I guess."

"Good! And, we're off!" Kaleen chuckles to herself.

"Off... what?" Elizabeth said.

Nobody talked.

Elizabeth started humming the tune to The Wizard of Oz.

"Why The Wizard of Oz?" Kaleen said.

"I dunno, cuz it uses the term, 'we're off'."

"Yeah… okay…"

No one talked until we were with Alex.

We came to the chocolate fountain, where Alex was dunking a strawberry into the dark, creamy, rich chocolate that made my mouth water.

"Mmmmm. That chocolate looks amazing!" I said. Really, I couldn't help it! It looked so rich!

"Want to try it?" Alex asked me eating his own strawberry. "It is really good," Now the chocolate was spreading all over his mouth!

"I thought you'd never ask!" I said, grabbing a strawberry with my bare hands. "Yum!" I said while I ate it. I only drizzled a little chocolate on it, not like Alex. He dunked it in! My stomach could not hold that, I knew.

"Oh! Hi, Elizabeth. I didn't see you," Alex said, looking up from his chocolate-covered strawberry. His face still had chocolate on it, so I picked up a napkin off the table and dabbed my face with it as an example. He didn't get it the first time, so I had to say, "You got a little…" my voice trailed off.

"Oh," he blushed and smiles at Elizabeth, causing her to blush.

"We'd love to stay and chat, but…" My voice trailed off yet again.

"What? We can stay and chat, Haylie," Seth's face twisted in a confused look. "Can't we?" he confirmed. I kicked him under the table and when he said, "Oh!" everyone looked at him. "Oh! I just remembered that… that I really wanted to talk to Matt about something. Can you come with me, guys?" he asked trying to help the situation.

"Um, I wanted to stay and… OUCH!" Seth had kicked Kaleen, I knew, and she quickly recovered by saying, "Um, these stupid chairs. They always make them too tall. I scooted in and… wham! I hit the table. Well, I can't just stay here sitting in these stupid chairs. I think I'll go with Seth and Haylie," Kaleen said.

"Yeah, I'd better come too," Elizabeth said.

"No! Um… Lizzie, can I see you… over here?" I motioned with my head to the wall.

"Lizzie," she said getting up and setting the napkin on the table. "I like it."

"What are you doing? You need to stay here with Alex! That's the whole point of us leaving! We were supposed to leave you ALONE! Alone with Alex!" Almost every word I said, I emphasized with speaking louder.

"Haylie… I really appreciate… what I'm saying is… can we go outside?" she stuttered.

"Okay. Let's go outside," We walked out and I mouthed the words, "I'll be right back!" to Seth and he nodded. I knew he understood.

"Okay," she said. "I really appreciate what you guys are trying to do for Alex and me, and yes, I really do like him, but I just don't really like being alone with him or anyone else for that matter. If you guys stay with me, I'll stay! If you want to leave, I want to come with you. Please, just trust me."

"But what about the dance a while ago? You danced with him and ended up falling in love! You've already passed the hard part of breaking the ice. Just dance with him and I promise it'll be fine. If you have any problems, just tell him you don't feel comfortable alone or dancing with him and come to me. He'll understand. He's a great guy," Firing back her excuse right to her, I gave her a bunch of excuses to dance with him… PLUS EXAMPLES! Extra credit.

"No. I can't."

"You can and you will. If I can do it with Seth, you can do it with Alex because they're both good guys. Except, Seth is even greater!" I said.

"Not true! Alex can do anything Seth can do, just BETTER!" She suddenly got aggressive with me.

"Ha! See? Already, you're defending him. You like him!" I added, "A lot!"

"Hey!" She giggled and playfully hit me on my arm. "Okay, but any problems, and I am coming to you… even if you're dancing with Seth or something."

"Don't worry," I agreed, "Seth and I are gonna stay close to you guys as much as we can!"

"Good," she paused. "Shall we?" she and I were arm-in-arm when we reached our table. "We're back!" She announced. "Well, um… Elizabeth? Can I ask you something… over there?" Alex gestured over to where I had before when Elizabeth and I were talking.

She rolls her eyed and took a breath, "Sure," she didn't want to be rude… or break our pact, I knew.

Chapter Fourteen

Elizabeth and Alex's Conversation

"**W**ELL, HERE, HAVE A SEAT," he pulled out two chairs for him and Elizabeth. "Okay, here's the deal," he spoke again, regaining confidence. "I'm sort of really nervous, and I know you probably are too, but the other dance a while ago… it wasn't hard to ask for you to dance, but now, it seems impossible."

She just nodded, so he continued.

"And… you're gonna have to help me with this one. Will you say yes?" he tried.

"Depends. Will you ask me properly?"

"Here goes nothing," he continues, "Elizabeth Campbell, might I have this dance?" his voice was shaky, but it was effective. A slow song filled the gymnasium.

"I… uh… I dunno. Sure," Her voice appeared almost shakier.

"Yes!" Kaleen shot up from the table with her fist balled in the air. When Elizabeth and Alex looked at her confused, she smiles and calmly says, "I'm gonna go see how Nick's doing," And wanders off. To refresh your memory, Nick is the boy who asked Kaleen to dance on the night of the last dance. I waved to her as she trotted towards Nick and her happy expression changed to angry. She had seen Nick with Ashley! Ashley!!! Was he cheating?

Kyle, KALEEN, AND ASHLEY'S CONVERSATION:

"Kyle," Kaleen tapped his shoulder. "Hi. Ashley? Oh, hey," she was trying to NOT blow up. "What are you doing here?"

"Um, it's kind of a dance... for the whole grade."

"Right..." Kaleen said.

See, Ashley and Kaleen have always been enemies. In second grade, Ashley pulled Kaleen's hair and Kaleen "got even" with her by putting glue all over her seat. They've been enemies ever since. That's what I was told, at least.

"So... what do you wanna do tonight?" Kyle said.

"Eat? Dance?" Ashley said.

"Okay... but I was sort of talking to..." She pointed to Kyle.

"Oh. Well, I was going to ask, anyway... if..." Ashley said.

"If...?" Kaleen said.

"I was wondering if we could let go of the past and become friends. I mean, what's it

I nodded in response. Walking back to Seth, I said, "Well, now that they're gone..."

"I don't mind them," He interrupts.

"What I mean is... well, now we're alone."

"Oh. That's true, I guess," he did NOT sound nervous.

I nodded. I was a little nervous, I realized. Thinking about Kaleen and Elizabeth so much, I never thought about myself.

"So," I started. "Would you like to dance?" I soon realized that my voice was shaky.

He shrugged and answered, "Sure."

We walked onto the dance floor and I realized he was a great dancer! I, however, was not so great. Let's just say I wasn't exactly headed for a dance future...

"Hey! You're doing great," he lies.

"You're not so bad yourself," I tried to sound official. I giggled. "No. You're great. I'm a klutz."

"Maybe you are, but for a klutz you're okay," he says.

"Ha!"

"No, really," He says and then smiles.

I smile back, "You're so awesome. You even tell lies just to make me feel better about myself. Seriously, you're the best."

Ten Minutes Later...

"Whaddya say? Want to hit the snack table? I hear there are more exotic foods this year. They even have sushi!" Seth looks hungry.

"Sure," I was almost positive I was as hungry as he was. We piled our plates up with pretzels, sushi, salad, mini finger sandwiches, (tuna, turkey, and ham!) and there was a little deli platter with different meats. I picked some turkey! Yum! As for drinks, there was lemonade, Coke, Pepsi, Sprite, pink lemonade, water, and root beer. Filling my glass to the rim with root beer, I snuck a little sip! "Mmmmm. This is good. Is this homemade?" I asked, as I tasted the sushi.

"No!" A girl cried. "Store bought. That's an insult to my mother's cooking!"

"Oh, well I'm sorry... I guess. I'm sure your Mom's cooking is just as good," I tried. Didn't work.

She shook her head angrily at me and trotted off with two other girls, snickering and pointing to random 6th and 7th graders.

"Bye Sammie!" Seth cupped his hands around his mouth and yelled over the blaring music.

"You know that girl?" I asked.

He nods. "It's Becca's friend," Beep! Seth's phone beeps once. Twice. Three times.

"Maybe you should get that!" I laughed. "The person must be eager..." My voice fades.

"It's Rosie and your sisters!" He laughs.

"What do they say?" I wondered.

"They say 'Hey, Hay and Seth. How r u doing? C u later!'" He pauses. "They're so cute!"

"Let me say something," I grabbed the phone. "Sorry," I said apologetically when I realized I had really snatched it hard. He nodded in response. I figured he was alright, so I wrote to Kate, Sarah, Cole, and Rosie:

Hey, guys! How are you doing? Seth and I are fine. Thanks
for checking in on us, anyway, though. I love you guys…
even Rosie. You're all just SO CUTE! Luv ya,
Haylie.

"What did you write, Haylie? Hey what did you write?" Seth was already pestering me. I can't blame him, though. It was his phone.

"Here," I handed it to him, "Give me the, 'okay' and I'll send it."

"Send," he read it over.

"What?"

"This is the 'okay'. You can send it," He agrees.

"Send," I said as I pressed the key that read, send.

"Cool. Let's go talk to Kaleen and Ashley," He suggests.

I was really surprised. He was suggesting talking to a couple of girls! Wow, he's sweet! I suddenly felt my face growing red. I was blushing! I quickly blinked myself out of that pause, realizing it was rather a long one. "Oh. Are you sure?"

"Why wouldn't I be?" he looked surprised.

"They're… they're girls!"

He shrugged. "Don't care. I don't mind. They make good conversation."

"Wait," I kind of jumped to conclusions, I admit it. "Do you like Ashley? Or Kaleen. Do you like Kaleen?"

"No!" He exclaimed. "No way. I… don't really mean to sound cruel or mean, like they're not good-looking. They are. I don't like them, though. I… well; I kind of like… someone else," He squinted.

"What?!" I demanded. I realized that I was tapping my foot, impatiently. "Who?" I calmed myself down, talking a long breather. "Whew!" I let out a gasp. The breath was a little too long.

"Well," he started. "I don't really…"

"Who?" I interrupted him. I tapped my foot some more. "Who? Who? Who?" I was beginning to sound like an owl.

"Okay, owl," He read my mind. "I…"

"WHO DO YOU LIKE!?" I screamed so hard, I had to plug my ears; afraid I had just broken his eardrums. I was afraid, also because I thought that the whole gymnasium had their eyes locked on me, but I didn't care.

"Sorry. I'm really eager, I guess."

"Ya like gossip?" he tries to change the subject.

"No. Just eager," I shot back. "Who?"

"Fine! I... um... I've sort of always had a major crush on... on you," He gave in.

"What? How could you do that? And here we are on a date! Oh, you're so... wait. What did you say?" Oh my gosh, I totally heard him say my name! Wow!

"Yeah. Not Kaleen, not Ashley, not Elizabeth, not one other person," He is so sweet!

I let out a gasp. "You... I..." I sputtered. I let out another gasp, and then jolted forward. I let out a startled cry as I landed headfirst into the punch bowl!!! Someone had pushed me! "Oh my gosh," I spoke first. Most of the gymnasium now had their eyes locked on me.

"Oh, wow! What can I... help! We need some help here!" Seth tries. "Anyone?"

A voice says, "Oh, no... I'm uh... busy. Pshaw. You know I'm not busy! But, you're not getting my help."

"Oh, that's real nice," I said. "I'm going to help you!" Seth shot back. Then he turns to me, "Haylie, let's get you some wipes. Let's just go home," he suggests.

"No! We came to have fun. Real, live, actual fun! Don't worry. I'll be out in ten minutes. I'm just going to clean off. No worries! I'm okay!" I denied his suggestion.

"Well, I don't know. I think we should just go now," By the time Seth was finished talking, Elizabeth, Alex, Kaleen, and Ashley came running over to me, all saying, "Oh, Haylie! Are you okay? What happened?"

"Nothing. I'm fine. Really," I assured them

"Hey. I'm really sorry," A guy with a football clutched under his arm apologized. "I didn't mean to hit anyone."

"That's okay. Don't worry about it," I assured him this time.

Three more boys came walking up to me, apologizing. Crazily, one of them said, "I'll make it up to you. How about I take you out for a night? Or pay for a week's worth of lunch money? I can do that!" he said. He was black and was wearing a jersey with gold, puffy pants. Weird. Oh, yeah! It was themed olden days! And he was a football player. Funny.

"No! I said I was fine! I'm just going to the shower rooms and I'll wash my hair! I brought a change of clothes, so I won't have to wear my stained dress," I assured them all.

"Okay. I'm really, really, really sorry!" Another said. They all shook their heads, agreeing.

"Wait! I have to tell you…" He explains that he was backing up to catch the football when he backed up too far and into me. So that's why I tripped, I thought.

Ten or Twenty Minutes Later…

I had showered and changed into my clothes. By the time I was finished with that and had danced with Seth for another twenty minutes, his Mom arrived with Rosie, Kate, Sarah, Ashley, and Cole in the car. She wanted us to get in! We would NOT fit, I could tell. Much to my surprise, we did. And the car was full. Good thing Seth's Mom had an SUV! That was a lifesaver!

"So," Mrs. Stone asks. "How was it? Good?"

"Well… the first half was…" Seth explains what had happened, from start to finish.

"Oh my! Are you okay? Do you need to wash up? Do you need a towel? Punch, was it?" she instantly starts asking questions.

"Yes, I'm fine. I've already washed up. No. No towel. I showered, already. Yes, punch. Punch, root beer, and ham," Then I moaned, "I hate ham."

When we arrived home, my mom wanted to know every little detail. "Tell me everything from start to finish!" She said.

"Everything?" I asked.

"Yes, everything," she insisted.

"Okay. Well, we enjoyed it, I guess. Seth has a little sister, Rosie. Kate and Sarah played with her for hours straight, I was told. Cole played with Seth's action figures," I started.

"Oh. Good. So they had a great time. What about you?" she said.

I had to tell her the whole thing, didn't I? Awww. Really, I just wanted to ditch this conversation and sleep. Skip this conversation, skip Texting Time, and skip everything. Just… needed… to… SLEEP! So, I started to tell her. "The first half was good…" I copied Seth's words. I explained the rest to her just as Seth had explained it to his Mom.

"Well, are you okay?"

"Yeah, Mom."

"Hurt?"

"No, Mom."

"Dirty?"

"No, Mom," she then made a confused face, so I explained. "I went straight to the shower rooms."

"All clean?"

"Yes, Mom. All clean," I just wanted to SLEEP!

"Want salad? You look starved!" She asked.

"No. I ate already."

"Whaddya eat?"

"Sandwich, salad, turkey, sushi, cookies. Plenty full, thank you," I explained and listed the foods I ate.

"Oh. You should sleep," she suggests.

"Yes! I think I'm really tired. It's already..." I paused to pull my phone out of my purse. I clicked on and waited for it to say, "Power on. Type password," It always said that when I turned it on. It did this time, too. "Power on. Type password."

"Ha!" My mom laughed. "Cool. How do I get that on my phone?"

"You don't. It was only on my phone when I got it. Ask the Verizon guy," My phone turned on. "It's almost 10:00. Good night and good riddance!" I ex-claimed

Chapter Fifteen

The Next Morning

When I awoke, I looked at the time. 7:16. I only had twenty or thirty minutes to get ready for school, since school started at 8:00 and it took ten minutes to get there.

"Oh, no," I moaned. "You're kidding me. I've got to get myself an alarm clock!"

It was my job to wake my siblings every morning. I started down the hall. My sisters shared a room. My brother had his own, downstairs. "Wake up," I said. I was a little sleepy, myself.

"What? School is today?" Sarah asked with a scratchy voice. Her voice was always scratchy in the morning. "It's Monday?"

I nodded. "Wake up, Kate. It's Monday!"

"Nooo!" She moans. "I want to sleep!"

"Sorry," I shrugged. "You can tell Mom that. I can't help anything."

"Oh!" Sarah screeched. "Owww!"

"Huh?" I asked as she pulled out a Barbie from under her back.

"Ouch!" She said.

I laugh, "Okay, now even Barbie… what's her name?"

"Rosie," Kate said.

"Now even Barbie Rosie says to wake up. I still have to wake Cole and I'm not quite sure Sabrina's awake. Wake up!" I said. They didn't budge. "Oh, fine!" I gave in. I held my hands in the air. I picked up Kate, then Sarah. "You will not go back to bed. Here," I set out two shirts: one with pink flowers, one blue with pictures of pretend fireworks. Then, I gave them a pair of shorts and a pair of jeans. I gave them each ballet flats to match. "Be dressed by the time I come back," I left the room.

"Haylie! Are you awake?" Sabrina asked.

"Yeah! Can you wake Cole?" I shouted down the staircase.

"Already did," she said.

"Okay," I yelled back as she finally came into view. "Did Mom cook?"

"No; cereal today."

"Okay! Be down in a minute."

I walked into my room and applied my makeup. Only blush and eye shadow, though, to make it faster. I curled about ten pieces of hair and turned off the curling iron.

"Ready?" Sabrina called up to me.

"Almost!" I yelled. I checked on Sarah and Kate. They were dressed. "Good," I praised them. "Ask Sabrina if she can make your lunch."

"Okay," Sarah said. "Sabrina!" She called downstairs.

"Sabrina? Is Cole ready?" I screamed.

"Almost!" She screeched.

I ran into the guest room, where Kevin slept. "Kevin? Can you drive us? I don't think Mom's awake and Dad's at work."

"Nooo," he moaned. "Too tired." He was still in bed.

"Then drink coffee!" I suggested. "C'mon!"

"No!"

"Yes! Drink coffee!" I suggested again, louder, this time.

"No! I'm too tired to get up."

"That's what coffee's for!" I yelled.

"Fine!" he yelled back. "Go away and tell me when you're ready."

"Thanks!"

Ten to Fifteen Minutes Later...

"Kevin? I'm ready!" Everyone was ready. We were waiting on Kevin. "Hurry!"

No response. I saw him running downstairs. "We're taking Mom's car," was all he said. Yes. That's it.

We all rushed into Mom's beautiful Bentley. Kate, Cole, Sarah, Sabrina, and I hopped into the car. Kevin was in no hurry, it was clear. "Kevin, step on it," I said.

"I'm going as fast as I can! Calm down!" He paused. "Whose school am I going to first?"

"Mine. Sabrina and I go to the same school," I responded.

"Where is that?"

"Colina," Sabrina answered before I could.

"Okay. Where do they go?" he asks motioning to Kate, Cole, and Sarah.

"Westlake Elementary. It's a few streets away from Oldcastle place," I said. He had a friend who lived on Oldcastle place. "You'll see it. The kids know where it is," I insisted.

"Okay."

"Going out with Kristy again?" I asked.

"How'd ya know?" He looked surprised.

"How could I not?" I rolled my eyes. "You're together almost 24/7," I took a long breath. "I miss you, Kev. We always used to play together... and practically obsess over board games and be together for hours! What happened to that?" I sounded as disappointed as I was.

"I don't know. I grew up. When are you going to do the same?" he says.

"Never. I never ever want to grow up, Kevin. Kristy is just a dumb obstacle getting in the way of us being together."

"Kristy is NOT stupid," he said.

"I know, but she's getting in the way of us! I would just get rid of her, if I were you," I insisted as we drove up to the parking lot of Colina.

He stopped the car, "You're welcome. Here's your lunch money, princess," he handed Sabrina and me each a $5.00 bill. "We'll talk later. Maybe after dinner, but I am not getting rid of Kristy! You're just plain spoiled. You want me all to yourself."

I exploded. Completely blew up. "I really hope you're kidding. I haven't seen you in years! Ages! I am not spoiled and I am certainly not selfish! Take it back!" I didn't wait until he responded, just walked away through the parking lot.

"Kevin," I heard Cole say. "Is Haylie spoiled?"

"Completely spoiled," he drove away, faster than usual.

Inside Colina Property

"Haylie!" A voice said.

Seth!

"Oh, hi."

"Yeah," He paused. "Well, last night was really fun."

"Very fun," I nodded.

"Just wanted to say 'hi'," he said.

"Hi," I said.

"I have to go. I'm gonna be late for class. History," he said.

"Oh, okay. Bye," I said.

I realized I was very hungry.

Oh, speaking of lunch, I should probably tell you about it. Well, I sat next to Kaleen and Nikki. Other people at the table included Alex, (who Elizabeth was talking to for literally the whole lunchtime) Seth, Elizabeth, and a few other people. Well, since Kaleen just had to say, "So, Ashley. Who do you like?" It started a whole conversation about crushes. I felt totally comfortable talking about it with friends, but with boys at the table? That is a little too much.

Ashley responded, "I dunno. I kind of like Alex, I guess. He's cute."

Elizabeth gasped at that comment. "What? Who?"

"Me," Ashley raised her hand, "You can't have him all to yourself."

"Yes I can."

Ashley rolled her eyes at that. "Whatever."

"Whatever to you, too," Elizabeth said.

"Shhh," Ashley started getting mad.

"What? Did you just tell me to shhh?" Elizabeth lost it. "You shhh!"

"No," Ashley rolls her eyes and stares at Elizabeth hard, "I didn't tell you to shhh. A cat did," she laughed like it was the most hilarious joke in the world.

"Shhh!" Elizabeth says, leaving the table to sit at another. Alex and Bailey followed. I could tell she was really annoyed.

So whose side was I on? Neither. Elizabeth totally overreacted, but Ashley shouldn't say she likes Elizabeth's crush, especially since he likes her too. What I don't like about Elizabeth is that she's a little too sensitive. She gets her feelings hurt over things like me hanging out with another friend. "Why would you hang out with her? Do you not like me anymore?" she would always ask.

But, I would rather be sensitive over being bratty any day. Ashley could be very annoying, no doubt about it. She would think that she's too cool to hang out with "level one freaks". See, to her, there are five levels:

1: No friends. People make fun of you. Example: Gary Simpson.
2: You're okay. You have only one or two friends. Example: Jeffrey Stewart.
3: You've got a few friends. Not very popular... but getting there. Example: Alexandra Melvin
4: Popular. You hang out with level 5 kids, but you never are cool enough to call them or anything like that. Example: Aly Nielsen.
5: Very cool. You earned your place with the cool kids and are hanging out with them constantly. Example: Seth.

Of course, Ashley rates herself as a level-fiver.

And unless you want to learn geography and science... and you probably don't, let's move on.

So, when I got home—Mom drove me; she finally woke up—Dad was sitting on the couch watching football. Home early, I guessed. "Home early?" I said aloud.

"Oh, no! C'mon, guys! Go! And... TOUCHDOWN!" He jumped up and did a little dance. "Good job!" He turned to me, "Oh. Hi. How was your day?"

"Good," I laughed. Then I repeated, "Home early?"

"Yes," his eyes didn't move from the T.V.

I set my backpack down on the kitchen table and came back into the living room. I slouched down onto the couch, "Who's playing?"

"Eagles versus Giants. Good game so far. Giants are winning by four points."

"Oh," About 15 minutes into the game, I snuck out, because I was getting very bored.

"Honey! Honey, come here!" My mom's voice echoed through the house (our house was fairly big). Sabrina and I rushed into the kitchen at the same time: me through the living room, her just coming downstairs. "Yeah?" she calls.

"Would you guys want to peel some potatoes?" she asks.

"Sure, but… why?" I ask.

"Thanksgiving, duh," Sabrina said. "You have a calendar. Use it."

I stuck my tongue out at her and she made a face back at me.

"Yes or no?"

"Sure," Sabrina and I responded at the same time.

"Good," my mother said. "Now I only have two peelers and I'm going to be peeling too, so we'll need another," she turned to me, expectantly, "Please go ask Miss Downer if she has a spare potato peeler, Haylie?"

Before I could answer, Sabrina volunteers, "I will!" Then she mumbles, "I need some air anyway. Stupid house. Someday, we'll need to crack a window or something."

I giggled at that.

"What are you laughing about," my mother asks.

"Nothing… So, I forget how to peel. It's been, like, a year. Can you show me how?"

"Yes," my mother said, "But can we wait until Sabrina gets back? I don't want to show it twice."

"Okay," I agreed. I looked around and suddenly noticed I was hot. Sweating. "Whew! Hot in here," I exclaimed.

"Let me turn the heat down. Maybe your father turned it up," she says.

While I was waiting for Mom to come back and Sabrina to return with the peeler, I hummed to myself. I realized I was still hot. "Mom? You turned it down?"

"Yes," she said. "Still too hot for ya, huh?"

"Yeah," I waited until I heard her coming downstairs and then said, "Thank you."

"Welcome. Oh gosh, I——" Her voice was cut off by the sound of the garage door slamming.

I waited, and waited. I was patient as I could ever be. I kept waiting. "Where are they?" I asked to myself. I flipped out my cell phone and punched in Sabrina's number.

"Hello," her voice said through the other line. "Who's this?"

"Me."

"Me? Me who?"

"Me Haylie!" I rolled my eyes. Oh no! I was slowly-but surely – becoming more and more like Ashley!

"Oh. It's you," she didn't sound happy. "Whaddya want?"

"Where are you? Mom and I have been waiting for twenty minutes. Literally! Are you coming home? Did you get the peelers?"

"No," I could picture her rolling her eyes. "Why?"

"'Cause Mom said to!" I said.

"Oh, that," I could hear a muffling sound. "That's not important. What's important is that Jordan Blacker just said 'hi' to me. I'm freaking out!"

"Really? How popular is he?" I bit my lip, "You know what? Don't answer that. Just… where are you?"

"Mall," she answers. "Why?"

"Why?" I repeated her. "Why? You know why!" I practically screamed, and took the phone from my ear. Trying to calm down, I put the phone back to my ear. "You were supposed to get the peelers."

"Peelers? Why on Earth would you need peelers?" she pretends.

"Potatoes! Ring a bell?"

"No," says Sabrina, "Not at all."

"Potatoes! You know? Thanksgiving potatoes!" I said.

"Oh yeah. I think I remember Mom saying something about that…" she says.

"Are you crazy? Oh my gosh. We were just talking about… I've gotta tell Mom."

"No! You can't! Mom… one second, Jordan. Little sister. She's really bugging me."

"Me bugging you?" I said.

"Yeah," she says.

"Oh my gosh… just go on," I sighed.

"Mom doesn't know I'm here! I told her I would get the peelers, but Sidney and Cassidy were going to the mall. They invited me! I couldn't say no," she explains.

"Why couldn't you?" I ask.

"Hello. Mall!" She says like it's obvious. "Whatever. So, I'm here now. Mrs. Landon drove us," she paused. "Oh please! I need a favor."

"What?" I say as my eyes widened.

"Please cover for me! Mom doesn't know I'm here!"

"Dude!" I say, in a loud whisper.

"Everything alright in there?" my dad called from the living room.

"Yeah, Dad," I move the phone away from my ear. "Fine."

He nods and waves. And mouthed the words, "Love ya."

"Love ya too," I mouthed back. And I put the phone next to my ear. "I'm sorry. I can't cover for you,"

"Why not? Give me one good reason," she demands. "One," she repeats.

"Well," I started. "I… I don't know, okay? I just can't."

"Good. So you'll do it?" she asks.

"No," I say.

"Two dollars."

"No."

"Three?" she says, expectantly.

"No! Unless you'll give me $20.00…" I say.

Then she interrupts, "Deal."

"Okay. I have to go. I think Mom is coming," I said. I was pretty rich. Already, I had $346.00 in pocket money… counting the $20.00 is $366.00! Yes!

"Bye," she clicked off.

I clicked off.

"Honey. Are the peelers here?" My mom's voice echoed through the house.

"Um, yeah. They're upstairs in my room. I'll get them!" I called into the hall.

Slipping a jacket, I ran across the street and ran up to Miss Downer's home.

"Hello," a cheery voice said sweetly. "Who's there?"

"Haylie," I said.

"Oh Haylie, darling! I knew you'd come, but I expected you sooner. You need the peelers?" says Miss Downer.

"Yes," I said. I thought to myself, how did she know?

"Oh, alright. I think I have a couple in my kitchen drawer... oh here they are! How many will you need?"

"Two," I said.

"Okay. Just bring them back when you're finished! Have a very happy Thanksgiving," said Miss Downer.

Nodding, I said, "You too," and then walked off. Really, I wanted to know what she was doing for Thanksgiving, but I knew I had no time for that. She had a husband and three kids. She had a very nice life, in my opinion. She will spend it with family, I guessed. For a forty nine-year-old, she looked really good. She was pretty and petite, and a very nice lady. Her real name was Alice. Alice Downer. I liked that name, Alice.

When I walked into my house a minute later, Mom was standing over the sink washing the potatoes. "Oh, hi," she said.

"Hi," says Dad from the living room.

"Hi," I say, acting like there was nothing to hide. Fortunately, Mom and Dad weren't too good at noticing something was, "up," so Mom just responded, "Come here. I'll show you how. Sabrina? Wanna help?" Mom calls upstairs.

"Um," I cover. "She told me she wasn't up for it. She felt like going to sleep. She doesn't want anyone to disturb her, though. She seemed very tired."

"Oh. Okay. I guess it's just you and me, kiddo," she says happily. I love my mom. She always works hard and does her best to keep the house clean and feed us and to do the chores and everything. She's a good Mom. So, I decide to just nod.

Thirty Minutes Later...

Mom and I were done with peeling the potatoes and had already mashed them and everything. They were in the oven next to the turkey. The cranberry sauce and gravy were done. I couldn't wait! They all looked so yummy.

"Haylie. Owww! Haylie come here NOW!!! Haylie! OWWW!" Someone screamed my name.

"Ugh," I rolled my eyes and put down the book I was reading, To Kill a Mocking Bird. "Coming. Where are you?"

"My room!" Then I heard another, "OW!"

Instantly, I knew it was Cole or Sarah or Kate. I wasn't sure which one, so I said, "Who is this?"

"Sarah! OW!" She screamed in pain.

Running into her room, I tripped two or three times, but never stopped. There she was. Kate's face was filled with horror and with tears dropping from her eyes. She was sitting next to Sarah.

"What happened? Sarah, are you okay?" I asked.

"Nooo!" she wails.

"What happened, Kate?" I moved my eyes to Kate expectantly. "What happened," I repeated.

"Sarah fell and hit her head on the side of the bed. She started screaming, 'Get Haylie!' so I called for you. She called for you. We called for you," Kate explains.

"Oh no! Sarah, you alright?" I said, worriedly.

"Nooo!" she wails, even louder.

"Let me go get Mommy, okay?" I said.

"I want to come!" she screams.

"Me too," says Kate quietly. "I wanna come too."

So, I held Sarah in my arms and Kate trailed slowly behind with tears in her eyes. "Kate? How bad was it?"

"Very, very bad. I heard the loudest thud I've ever heard in my life. If it was a minor injury, I wouldn't be crying, would I?" says Kate.

"Guess not," I agree. Dad and Kevin were in the living room, so we told them. Shortly, they were trailing behind us, too. Cole had heard Sarah's screams, so he came right along behind us. We all walked into Mom's room, all six of us.

Her face was sad and twisted by the time we were done explaining.

"I'll take her to the hospital," Kevin had said. Mom was too sad to speak. She just stared at Sarah and examined her head for bumps.

So my dad said, "I'll come. Honey? You coming?"

"Yes," That was all she said. "Yes, I'm coming." No comments, nothing.

My dad said, "Haylie, you'll need to watch Cole and Kate while we're gone."

"Okay," I said. I felt her head. Sure enough, there was a huge bump on the back of her head. "Ouch!" She kept saying, "Ouch!" and crying loudly.

My mom immediately grabbed a coat. "I have the keys. Let's go—fast."

Nodding and taking Kate and Cole by the hand, I slowly walked upstairs.

"Is Sarah going to die?" Cole asks. "Is she?"

"Oh, Cole," I said. I didn't honestly know. If the bump was that bad, she could die, but if she was going to die, I would think she'd die instantly, and she's still alive. I thought she was going to get hurt pretty badly, though. Kate had even said that the bump was extremely big and she hit it hard. I was positive she wouldn't die! So I laughed and answered, "Oh, Cole. No!" My voice softened, "But she still might be hurt pretty badly."

"Why not?" Cole looked confused. "Why won't she die?"

Shrugging, I said, "I know it couldn't be that serious. If she were going to die, she would die instantly. She's still alive, isn't she?"

"I don't know, actually. What if she died?" he hung his head.

"Don't be silly. I'm 99.9% sure she's still alive. If she wasn't, don't you think Mom and Dad would have called us," I laughed.

"Well, okay," I could see Cole's expression (very, very sad) since he lifted his head.

Chapter Sixteen

B Y THE TIME MOM, DAD, Kevin, and Sarah came home, we were playing card games on the coffee table in the living room. We decided we should be closer to the door, and Kate didn't want to mess up her room, and Cole said 'no' immediately, so the living room seemed like the best choice since the coffee table was very wide. The game we were playing was called hand and foot. It's very interesting. No time to explain it, though. Oh, no! We have to move on with the story, don't we?

Okay, so Sarah was in Dad's arms, huddled into a ball.

"Ouch..." She groaned.

"The doctor gave her some anesthesia to let her sleep. She kept kicking and crying," My dad said, scratching his head. "I just can't bring my mind to think why they didn't do more than an x-ray," he shook his head. "Weird," says Dad.

"Honey, it's okay. She's already healing," she took Sarah from Dad's arms and says to her, "Honey? Are you awake? Wakey, wakey!"

"Huh? Where am I?" she was almost fully awake.

"Home, Sarah. Here... lie down," says Mom. She walks over to the couch and lays Sarah down. Kisses her, and then turns to us. We all had a crooked look on our faces. Then, we all started asking questions rapidly. "I thought the doctor gave her anesthesia!" "Why is it already wearing off?" And, "Sarah? Do you feel okay? How do you feel?"

"Guys! Shhh. I don't want to confuse her. One at a time, please!" Mom glared at us and said to Sarah, "Hello, honey! How do you feel?"

"Not too good. My head hurts… owww!" She groaned and held her head tightly. "Owww," she said again.

"Oh, I'm sorry, honey. Maybe do you want to lie in your bed? I'll bring up some chicken soup!" Mom said. She explains, "It's her favorite."

"Oh," Kevin nodded.

"Yes! Thanks, Mommy," Sarah exclaims. "Ohhh…"

"Oh, alright, then," Mom says. "Daddy? Take her upstairs, will you?" she said to my father.

He nodded, took her in his arms, and slowly walked her upstairs without saying anything more.

For hours, no one talked to each other. No one said a word. Everyone was alone, either talking to Kristy, sneaking cookies, or applying makeup. That is, until Mom called a family meeting in the living room. Don't get me wrong; we're not the kind of family who gets together all the time to work out our issues together and decide on things together. Oh, no! This "family meeting" thing is not on our usual schedule. Nope. But, since Mom called all of us into the living room immediately and said it was super-duper extra important, we all dropped what we were doing and rushed into the living room. When I entered the living room, Cole, Kevin and Mom were already there and Kate and Dad were skipping down the staircase, happily. That is, until they heard the news. What was this all-important "news"? Well, let me start from the very beginning, when I sat down in my living room chair.

So, I slouched down into my favorite chair. It was purple to match our living room theme and it was very cushiony. It's been classified as "my chair" since we moved into our old house. I had been just about to turn eight. My parents decided to another place, really far away from here. Then, I turned thirteen, and my parents again decided to move to this community (of course it wasn't a family decision; we NEVER had these kind of meetings!) because it was "A better community and way of living for us," At least that's what Dad said.

So anyway, I slouched into "my chair". My mom immediately started yapping away. "Okay. I hate to say this because we clearly don't need any more bad news or things to bring our stress level up, but I needed to tell you all this… well, this news urgently, so we can start at it soon," Pausing before she said anything else, she took her glasses case off the shelf and slipped them on. She pulled a sheet of paper from her back pocket and recited it to us. "$366.00 needs to be paid by

Thursday. Thursday! Now, how in the world could we do that?" she said. The energy in the room was bad. Sad, even.

Well, before Dad suggested, "How about we all work it off? Kevin can help Mrs. Sweeny across the street with chores. Haylie and Sabrina can do community work. Cole can help me with fixing cars and Kate can maybe do little jobs around people's houses! Mom can take care of Sarah and work from home."

"Wow," I was past surprised. How could he come up with that on the spot? Brilliant! Oh, well, his job is mostly to pitch ideas for the master chef. He's great! "Good job, Dad."

He laughed. "Oh, honey! Pitching ideas is really my job."

"I know. Sorry. Mom, go on," I said.

"Okay. That really is a great idea! All in favor say 'Aye'," My mom suggests.

"Aye" I agreed. I turned to Mom.

She said, "Aye"

"Aye" Cole said. Kate said, "Aye" also, but I don't think

"Me. Uh, I mean, aye," My dad corrected himself

"I do NOT!" Kevin declared. Everyone turned to stare at him. "I mean, as it is, Kristy thinks we aren't spending enough time together!"

Everyone groaned at that. That was a lie! He spent too much time with Kristy as it was!

"Kevin," my dad said. "If you want to stay in this household, you're going to have to commit. Commit! Help us raise money. A fundraiser! Anything! But, you'll need to commit either way," He scratched his head. "Or else find somewhere else to stay," he said.

Wow. No he couldn't possibly refuse. I mean, unless he had another place in mind, which I highly doubt, by the way.

He groaned. "Now that's a little harsh, don't you think?"

"Nope. Not at all," My dad seemed very calm. Was he serious? Was he actually going to kick Kevin out? I thought not, but he said, "I'm very, very serious," Well, now I'm positive!

That's why I was not surprised when Kevin responded, "Fine! Ruin my life, why don't you?"

"Well, I'm sorry, Kevin, but, unless you have another house in mind, there's no way I can let you stay for free. Now, your mother has more laundry to do, more cleaning to do, and an extra mouth to feed! It… it just wouldn't be… logical," my dad told Kevin with nothing but a stern look on his face. "I don't care! I'll call Kristy and ask her to help me——" Kevin hissed.

"No. Do not drag Kristy into this. It is a family… project, if you will," Dad interrupted.

"But——" Kevin was interrupted once again.

"No! Don't tell Kristy."

"Why not?!" Kevin screamed.

"Why does she need to know? What's the point?" Dad shot back.

"She might be able to help. We need help, anyway."

"No. A family project," Dad insists. "And we'll start tonight," she adds.

"What! No! Kristy's coming over to——"

"Cancel it," Dad said, plainly.

"What! No way," He sat back on the couch. "I'm an adult, now. I make my own decisions."

"You'll be an adult when you get your own house. For now, my roof, my rules," Dad said. "Period. No more discussion."

"Ugh!" Kevin grabbed my favorite pillow off of "my chair" and screamed into it. "Ugh!"

"Cut it out!" I snatched the pillow from him and sat on it. "Still wanna put your mouth on it?" I snapped.

No answer.

"Can we just get on with this meeting?"

"Fine. So the decision is made then: we're doing community work?" Mom said, as there was a knock at the door.

"I got it!" Cole yelled. Mom got up anyway and walked to the door with him. She opened the door.

And you'll never guess who was standing there!

Kristy.

It was about thirty minutes later when Kristy came downstairs giggling, clinging on to Kevin's shirt. "Ha! If only. She was totally rude to Megan. I mean, I would think, since they were sisters, she would be a little mean, but the way she acted… I just… oh, I don't know. She just wasn't being very nice. Megan was trying to fit in! I... I just don't know," Kristy was saying. "Oh! Haylie. How are you?"

"Good," Really, what else could I have said?

Kristy opened her mouth to say something. Kevin said it for her, "Well. You're doing well. Not good," Apparently, I could have said, "Well."

"Oh, you know me so well!" said Kristy.

Kevin responds with a kiss. Kristy laughs. "Ewww," I moaned. "Gross."

"What?" Apparently, Kevin heard me. "You mean this?" he kissed her again.

"Yes! Stop that!" I laughed.

"Kev. Haylie is getting grossed out, now," Kristy said.

No. Oh, no. She called Kevin Kev! That's my nickname for him. Not cool. Now, this was going a little too far. But (of course) I didn't say it aloud. Oh, no! Actually, I said, "Kev? Can I see you in private?"

"Haylie, you know whatever you can say to my face, you can say to Kristy," he denied. Obviously, he had no idea what the word private meant.

"No. Alone," I pulled him into the kitchen and made sure Kristy wasn't listening before I started talking. I told her, "Kristy, you can sit in the living room," she nodded, and I started talking to Kevin. "Kevin! She totally stole my nickname for you!"

"No."

"No? No what!?" I exclaimed.

"Share, Haylie. Share," Kevin said.

"Kevin! No. This is not fair! You're spending way too much time with Kristy. I mean, I like her and everything, but since you came, it's been, 'Kristy and I are going out tonight!' or 'Sorry. Busy. Plans with Kristy'. And, 'Kristy this', and 'Kristy that'! It's not fair to me. Or the family, for that matter!"

"I'm... sorry," Is all he said? Oh, gosh.

"Sorry? Sorry? Sorry won't mend broken dreams. Broken hearts!" I screamed.

"Who has a broken heart?" he demanded.

"No one... yet. Just, please tell Kristy I think she needs to back off sometimes. She's taking up too much time. Time we could be spending together. Tell her to leave, for all I care!" I said.

There was a sniffling sound. Then, a voice sounded. Hmmm. Oh! It was Kristy's voice. It was saying, "Fine! I'll leave, then!" The door opened... then closed. Oh, no! Wow. I just broke Kevin and Kristy up! Not good.

Kevin said, "Kristy! Wait!" Too late. And he knew it. That's why he turned on me, frowning, saying, "Fine, Miss Selfish Brat. Now, I will be free. Free and lonely! Don't count on me talking to you," he stomped upstairs. "Ever!" He screamed. I heard his door slam. I was… speechless. Simply speechless. And guilty. This was not good. I knew there was only one thing to do. Actually, there were a thousand things to do, but only one right thing to do: call Kristy.

And that's just what I did, three or four times.

Everything was going to be all right. I would call her and work everything out. Kevin would forgive me. Maybe, they would worship me. No, I seriously doubt that.

There was only one thing standing in the way of all of this talk about how everything would be well again.

She didn't answer.

The next day, I woke up right on time. It was Sabrina's turn to dress Kate and Sarah. Except… Sarah wasn't going to school. Her head wasn't fully healed; Mom and Dad were worried. So, Sabrina would dress Kate and Kevin would dress Cole.

When I was dressed and my hair was done, I ran downstairs and made Kate, Sarah, Cole, and Kevin. Why did Kevin need a lunch? He was starting work at Burger King, and he wasn't getting free food. I had to pack him a lunch, also. Great. It was even more time-consuming. Here's what I put in the lunches:

Sandwiches (peanut butter and jelly on white, tuna fish on wheat, and turkey and cheese on white.)
Ding Dongs (the little chocolate cake things.)
Fruit (apples, pears, bananas, and peaches.)
Juices (Capri Sun and Minute Maid)
Carrots (Cole's all-time favorite vegetable)
Cheese and crackers
Pudding

When I was done, I packed Cole, Sarah, Sabrina, and my backpack with books, homework, supplies, and lunches.

"Come on!" Sabrina yells. She mumbled, "You're gonna make me late… again."

"Shhh! You're gonna wake Sarah!" Kevin hissed.

"You shhh!" Sabrina shot back. Today was not her best day, I could tell. Her hair was messed up and she kept whining, "Gosh. Stupid hair… ouch! Jeez," Poor Sabrina. Been there, done that. Bad hair days are not my favorite day of the year.

Finally, we were all ready and my mom was fully dressed. She told us all, "Please get in the car. We need to be there on time! Sabrina has to be there early for a cheer practice. Kate has Speech at 8:15. Cole has gate testing in fifteen minutes and he can't possibly be late! We're on a tight schedule here, people."

We nodded and got into the car. My phone started ringing. The caller ID told me it was Seth. "Hi."

"Hey," he said. "You coming to school?"

"Yes. Be there in about ten minutes. Why?"

"I… just wanted to tell you something," He started.

"Oh. Ask me over the phone," I suggested.

"I can't. It's really private," he said and his voice was shaky.

"You sound sad," I started to pry.

"I'm not."

There was a long pause. Then, I asked, "What happened?"

"Nothing. I mean… something. But, I'm not telling you over the phone. Like I said, it's just too private."

"Well, okay. See you at school," I clicked off. Hmmm. I wondered what the problem was.

When I got to school, everyone was acting beyond odd. Weird. So, asked Nikki, "What happened here?" she said, "She… died."

"Who?" I had asked.

"Mrs. Bartelstone," she said, solemnly.

"What?! How?" I demanded.

"She… uh… had a heart attack," Even Nikki who almost never showed any emotion was frowning and tears were dripping from her eyes.

"No! She wasn't even that old!" I realized I was suddenly screaming. And lowered my voice. "When was this?"

"Just last night, I guess," Nikki replies.

"Hey! Haylie! C'mere!" Seth comes running at me. "I have to tell you some… really sad news."

"Nikki already told me."

"Dang! Nikki! You told me you'd let me tell her!"

She shrugged, "Sorry. She was asking for it… wait. Why would you want to tell her, anyway? Does someone like her?"

"Well, kinda," Seth blushed.

"Oooo!" Nikki said. "Someone's got a crush!"

"Yeah. And?" Seth said.

"And? What do you mean, 'and'? My point was: you like Haylie!"

"Yup. I do," He gave in.

"Awww. You're a good couple!" Nikki says.

"Shhh!" I hissed. "Don't have to tell it to the world!"

"Really?" she sneered. "Seth and Haylie sitting in a tree! K-I-S-S-I-N-G!!!" She turned to the schoolhouse and screamed.

"So much for not telling the world," Seth groaned.

"Well, good job trying to make Nikki go away," I said, moving on.

He stared at me, confused. "What?"

"Well, you told her you liked me. Nice way to make her go away," now, even I was confused. Wasn't he lying?

"Oh, I wasn't really joking. It's true," he said, blushing.

My breath caught in my throat. I liked him, too. I didn't think he was telling the truth! Hmmm. Guess he was. Then, I answered him. "Oh," Oh. Oh was practically all I could say. I mean, put yourself in my position. What would you do? Exactly.

"Well what did you want to tell me?"

"The news. The Mrs. Bartelstone news," he said.

"Oh. I already know that," I said.

"I know. Nikki said she'd let me tell you, but… whatever," He shuffled his feet and sighed, "Sad, huh?"

"Yup. Did the district hire a new teacher to sub?"

"Yeah. I think her name is… I don't know. I think her name is Mrs. Sunshine," he said.

"Oh! She sounds nice," I exclaimed.

"But, I'm not sure if that's her name," Seth told me. "I'm probably wrong," he reminded me.

"Well," I started, "if you're right… she seems very nice, then."

"Yes," He paused. "Would you like me to walk with you to class? I'm really eager to see Mrs. Sunshine or whatever her name is!"

Smiling, I answered, "I'd like that," and we walked off.

During the next few hours, we didn't do too much work. Mostly, our history teacher let us play games like hangman. She loved that game. Seth wasn't right: her name was Mrs. Stephenson. Not Mrs. Sunshine! Close… they both start with "S."

So, I bet you'd like to know what Seth said to me. Yeah? Well, it's kind of not your business… but if you MUST know. If you don't? Too bad. Let me replay it. Here's how it went:

Seth said, "So… how was your weekend?"

"Good, I guess. Nothin' fancy."

"Oh."

"Yeah…" I said to break the silence.

"Well, is your sister doing alright? You told me she hurt her head."

"Yeah. Yeah. She's doing… better… then she was a day ago," I said. She wasn't doing well, but she was doing better than she was yesterday, that was true.

"I have a feeling that still doesn't mean she's doing too well. Is she seeing things? Constantly screaming out?"

"No. I don't think—"

"Good. That would NOT be good at all," he said, breathing a sigh of relief.

And, that was pretty much it. By the time he stopped talking, I was at my locker. Nothing personal.

Well, when I was walking to the Colina parking lot, I heard Ashley yell my name, "Haylie!" She wanted to know if I could have her over until 4:30; when her Mom got back from the dentist. I said, "Sure. My mom probably wouldn't mind," And I was right, because as soon as I got home, I said, "Mom! Ashley's here," And Mom said, "Oh. Yes! Company. Good, well, now I have another person to help me eat all of my hot cider. I made a little too much," And she looked as happy as she was. I said, "Why would you make cider today? It's not even that cold."

"Yes. Well, I… felt like cider. Thought it would set the mood."

"What 'mood'?" I said.

"Cheery! I love cheery moods. Christmas is almost here! It's December 6th."

"Oh," I set my backpack on the table. "Sorry. She's… weird."

"It's okay. My mom is worse," Ashley added, "Much worse."

"Ha! Really?"

"You'll see. When she comes to pick me up, talk to her. She's nuts," Ashley pulled back her long, blonde hair into a ponytail and sighed. "Let's go in your room. I've never seen it."

"Okay," I led her up the stairs and into my room. "This is it. Not much."

"Yeah. It's almost nothing compared to my room. Your house is fairly big, though."

I nodded, "So, what's your homework for tonight?"

"Chemistry, math, social studies. My least favorite subjects, of course," she rolled her eyes.

"Oh, really? Don't you get good grades? Mr. Donavan always calls your name for examples and you never get the questions wrong."

"Yeah. I'm good at it. I just don't like it," she explains.

"Ah," Brushing my hair, now, I sighed. "Chemistry, math, and studying.

"Studying for what?" Ashley asks.

"Math. I really hate math."

"Me too," she nodded and asks, "Hey, do you think we can maybe have a snack? I'm hungry."

"Yes. Whaddya want?"

"Anything," says Ashley. "No allergies."

"Ah, me too," I set down my brush. "Come here."

"Kay," she said. "Do you… think Matt is cute?"

"What!" My eyes widened. "No way! Are you kidding! Ewww!"

"Oh. Pshaw! Me neither! Ewww," she lied.

"Lies! Lies!"

"Okay. Yeah. He's really cute. But he likes you. Not me. And I like him a lot!"

"Okay, okay. I'll ask him about you tomorrow and see what he says. Maybe at lunch," We were in the kitchen, by now. "Shhh! My brother and his friend will tease you about Matt. Don't let him hear you!"

Ashley had gone home and our homework was done. It was the next day. I had already gotten dressed, and Kevin was driving us to school: Kate, Cole, Sabrina, and me. When I was in chemistry class, I passed Matt a note:

```
Do you like Ashley?
```

He had sent me back:

```
No. You already know who I like.
```

And I wrote:

```
Me?
Yes.
But do you also like Ashley?
Why do you want to know?
Because!
Not really
Kinda! Do you like her? Yes or no?
Not really!
I know that. I'm asking what you think about Ashley!
I don't like her!
If I told you she liked you, would you like her?
Nope.
Oh, my gosh. I'll talk 2 u at lunch.
You're sitting with me at lunch?
No.
Oooo! You like me.
No I don't.
```

I crumpled up the notes and walked to the trashcan and threw them away.

Chapter Seventeen

At Lunch

I told my friends I had to ask Matt something; they accused me of liking him, and I told Ashley to explain the whole thing. She did, and I was off to the table Matt was sitting at. And, I still remember, still regret it. Friends of his were teasing Matt and me up until the point where I told them to get lost. Here's the conversation, if you're interested:

Me: "So do you like Ashley or not?"

Matt: "No."

Me: "But she likes you."

Matt: "I don't really care."

Me: "Okay, well that settles it."

Matt: "Good."

Then, I walked back to the table where Ashley was sitting, practically spazzing out. "What happened? What did he say?"

"He said no."

"Really! Wow," she said.

"Yeah, I'm really sorry."

"Whatever. I never really liked him anyway. I was just saying that to make him feel good. No one likes him! Ewww."

And…I thought I should tell you… there is one more person who I kind of like… WAY better than Seth. And. Since you aren't going to tell anybody, I can tell you. Here I go. His name is… Justin. Justin BIEBER!!!!!!!!!!!!!!!!

WHEW! Glad I got that out.

Later That Day In Chemistry Class:

Ashley sat next to me and since there was a lab experiment, I decided to pick Ashley as me partner so we could talk. When our chemical exploded (that was NOT supposed to happen), we had to duck under the desk and our teacher said that we had to start the experiment over. As we were groaning, Ashley noticed a weird shining… thing on the ground.

"Looks a lot like a coin… must be," she muttered. "Must be a coin…" She stood up and bent down to pick it up. When she came back up, I noted the odd coin. It was very shiny, gold. It was bigger than a nickel… smaller than a quarter.

"What is it?" I asked.

"I don't know… hey! Look at this! '1876, one quarter'. I wonder…" Her voice trailed off.

"Oh, wow! How in the world would it have gotten in a chemistry lab?"

"Is there a problem, ladies?" Our teacher was looking at us, now, along with the whole class.

"Oh. No, sir… we just found a coin from…" I looked at the coin again, "1876."

"Really? Would you like to show the class?" he looked interested. Before we got a chance to answer, he said, "Lemme take a look at that," And we showed it to him. "Ladies and gentlemen, I think," he continues, "I think we have a coin of quality here. An 1876 quarter," he smiled. "And as a teacher, I think it will be fair for you, as a student and someone who first found it, I have decided to let you be in possession of this lovely item," he said.

"English?" Ashley asks me for translation.

"He's going to let us keep the quarter," I said, smartly.

"Ah. Thanks, Mr. T."

"Well, it would only be fair," He sighed. "But... which one of you found it?"

"Me," she said at the same time I said, "Ashley did."

"Well, then, Ashley? You've got yourself a rare 1876 Canadian quarter, then. Now class, we will move on to the next step... and please try not to blow it up," The class giggles. "Now, if you would take your potion on the right and shake it, hard, without spilling. Now, observe what happens when you mix the two 'potions', as you guys like to call it. And, please stand back: You never know. It very well could blow up. So be careful! Careful!" he said as he wrote careful on the blackboard and underlined it three times. "Proceed," His voice was shaky.

The class poured and watched.

"Whoa!!!!!" The class exclaimed. "Look at mine!"

"Hmmm."

"Now get out your pen and chemistry pad. Note what happens, please," he said.

Most of the class was too caught up in what they were doing to listen to him, and plain ignored him.

"Um... is this supposed to be bubbling?" Alex said.

"Oh, dear. How bubbly is it, exactly?" Mr. T. asks.

"Very!" he said.

"Oh... lemme take a look at that, son... It's very, very bubbly How much carbon did you put in this!?"

"Two cups," he said calmly.

The class screamed and groaned and yelled at him.

"Alex! You were supposed to put in only two tablespoons!" Said Mr. T with a sigh. "Well, alright. Everyone duck!"

But I guess Ashley didn't duck in time, and the chemical exploded on her. "Ahhh!!!! Ewww. Gross. Get this off! I'm covered in... GET THIS OFF OF ME, MR. T!!!"

"Um... oh. Ashley! I'm so sorry, I... I should get this off of you."

"Okay, so what do I need to do? Jump in the school pool? Do one hundred laps of track?"

"Go to the nurse! Just go. Quickly, now," he said.

The class exploded into laughter after she was gone. Even I had a couple of giggles I needed to get out.

"Alright, class. That will be quite enough, now," he slapped his ruler against Alex's desk. "Now, you may be excused to pack your backpacks and get a head start waiting by the lot," He looked around to see thirty-six solemn faces. "Well what are you waiting for? GO!" I heard him mumble, "Rotten kids," and I laughed.

"But not you, Miss Carter. You will stay here."

"Excuse me? Did I do something wrong?" I asked, innocently. Honestly, I couldn't think of a thing I did wrong. What did he want with me?

"Please, Miss Carter. No questions."

"But——"

"No 'buts', Miss Carter. Now, I did teach your sister, Sabrina, and I know what she's like. And you, Miss Haylie, seem exactly as she is. And, if I'm right, you're a slacker," he rasped.

"Slacker… me?" I asked.

"Yes, Miss Carter. Now, before I give you a straight week of detention, I think it would be a good idea to come talk to me, don't you?" he said.

"Fine," I groaned.

"What?" he said.

"Fine!" I snapped.

"What?"

I looked up. He wanted me to address him. "Yes, Mr. T," And walked over to his desk.

"Now, I saw you laughing about Ashley's incident. And, that was not nice, Miss Carter, not nice at all. Especially since it looked that you were friends. I do not think it is right to mock your friends, Miss Carter, not at all! And after what you did, I should just punish you now, isn't that right?"

"No! I barely laughed! The whole class was——" I tried.

"Do not try to wriggle yourself out of trouble, Miss Carter! Don't test me! I taught your sister, and she was a slacker. Just like you are! And you are a poor-spirited child; you know that, Miss Carter? Principal Truman will be hearing about this! You should be ashamed!" His face turned red.

"I—"

"No! No more. Really, Haylie, do you think you can get away with this?" he said.

"Uh, Mr. ——uh Sir, I didn't... see, the whole class was laughing. I couldn't help it. I mean Ashley... Ashley is awesome and I didn't want to me mean, I couldn't help it. I'm sorry, Sir, but I won't take any blame for this. I was not the only one laughing. It's unfair."

There was a very odd silence. Awkward, for me. And... he SMILED! "Are you ready to debate about it?"

"What? Well, I'll debate anything if it's the truth!" I answered, smirking.

"Well, I can understand why you're right, Haylie! You did it! You got it!" He exclaimed.

"What? I've got what?" I pondered this.

"Haylie, would you like to be in the debate club?" he asked.

"What? Me?" I thought, why me? Was this whole thing a JOKE?

"Yes, you," he clapped, "good job. I think you might be good for the position!"

"What position?!" I stared at him.

"See, the debate team is looking for another member to join. I recommended you, and the president said that I needed to prove it. And, I did!" He smiled, eerily, taking a recorder out of his pocket. He pressed a button and I heard me saying, "I'll debate anything, if it's the truth!" And my mouth hung open in awe and shock. How dare he made a "fake" punishment for me, got me "fake" in trouble, and "fake" yelled at me! But, I couldn't argue because I remembered that my mom was waiting for me out front, probably wondering where I was.

"Um, thanks, Mr. T., but I have to go. My mom is wondering, probably, where I am, and..."

"So will you join?" Asked Mr. T.

"I... I don't know, Can we talk tomorrow?" By now, it was Thursday. I could talk to him tomorrow sure!

"Yes."

"Kay, bye."

"Bye," he said.

I raced to the parking lot where my mom was waiting, checking her watch.

"Haylie! Where have you been?!" she said. "School has been over for almost fifteen-minutes!"

"Sorry, Mom. I kinda got in… fake… trouble."

"What are you talking about?" she looked at me, weird. "Never mind. Just get in the car and then tell me."

I hopped in, "Fine. Okay, so Mr. T got me in fake trouble, and it turns out it was all a test for me."

"Test?"

"Yeah," I answered. "A test to see if I was debate team material."

"Oh."

"Oh?" I asked.

"Oh," she said. "As in did you get in?"

"Yes. But, I was going to ask you if I could… can I?" I asked.

"You want to?"

"Oh, I guess. I don't care."

"You would need to stay after school, sometimes," she said.

"Well, I don't know. I guess I like debating, sometimes," I said.

"Well, you certainly debate with your siblings, I can tell you that," she laughed. "No, seriously, if you want to, join! I don't care."

"Okay. I think I'm going to join," I said.

"Good. Another activity to keep you busy."

"Yeah," My phone rang, "I would catch a grenade for ya! Jump in front of a train, for ya!" It sang. That was my ring tone: "Grenade" by Bruno Mars. "Sorry, Mom, one sec," I answered it. "Hello?"

"Hi, Haylie. It's Ashley. I heard about the thing with Mr. T. Some people say you didn't turn in your homework. What happened?"

"Oh, he got fake mad at me, and it turns out it was all a test to see if I would fit an open position for the debate team."

"No way! Did you make it?" she said.

"Yeah."

"Oh. Well, anyway, I also wanted to ask you about something."

"Okay," I said. "Go ahead."

116

"Okay, so there's this… thing… like kind of like… well, a tryout… for a couple of things."

"Oh, cool. Want me to watch you tryout?" I asked. I really wasn't sure where this was going.

"No, not exactly. I was wondering what sport you like. You could try out for a few, if you want."

"Oh! What sports are you doing?" I ask.

"I don't know; whatever you're doing."

"Okay… I like… basketball. I like cheerleading… I like dancing… I like softball…," I suggested. And shrugged. "I don't care."

"Okay, you probably don't want to try out for too many, though. It's not like it's free."

"Okay."

"Let's do cheer and basketball?" she suggested.

"Okay! I'll ask my mom," I covered up the speaker. "Mom? Can I do… two sports?"

"Oh, honey, we're already struggling as it is. I don't think…"

"Please!!!! I'll pay for one sport entirely," I pleaded.

"Well, fine, but one sport is entirely your money."

"Thanks!" (Into the phone) "Okay, I'll do it."

"Great! Basketball is every Tuesday and cheer is every Monday. They're both at 3:30."

"Cool. Thanks." Hanging up the phone, I saw Mom's look and felt a lecture coming on.

"Sweetie, you know that we can't afford this! Even if you pay for it—"

"Mom, it's practically already paid for. I got it covered! Don't even worry," I said.

"Honey, but how will you pay for it?" she curiously stared at me. "Really, I don't know how you're going to——"

"Mom, I got it," I insisted.

"Well, okay, but only if you'll pay for the second sport," she slammed on the breaks. To be honest, my mom is not the best driver in the world. My dad is good, but want some advice? Never drive with my mom, unless you want to die. Literally. No, I'm kidding, she isn't really that bad. She is bad, though.

"Yes, it's fine," I sat back in my seat and held on to the handles.

"Is there something wrong?" she said.

"No, it's just… did you ever take driving lessons?" I smiled, innocently.

"Oh, no. My father said he wouldn't pay for it, and I had zero money. The only thing I could do was to teach myself. And I did."

"Oh, I see."

"What?"

"Nothing," I groaned as she forgot to put on her blinkers on and a loud horn arose from a car behind us. "Just… did you ever consider trying out a driving lesson now? I mean, when you do have money?"

"Oh, no. I'm fine. It's not like I need it," she stared at me hard and exclaimed, "Wait! You think I need a driving lesson!"

"Yes-er-no," I tried.

"Oh, honey…" she slammed on her brakes and I almost shot through the window, I swear. "Oh, I'm sorry! Maybe you're right."

For the rest of the ride, we were silent.

When I got home, my dad wasn't home, and my sisters were… running around. Together. My sisters were running around together! Sarah was okay! "Sarah! You're okay!"

"Yeah, Mommy took me and Kate to the doctor's office," she gleamed at me.

"Why Kate?" I asked.

"Kate wanted to come," My mom answered. "Sarah was missing school and Kate thought it wasn't fair that she had to go. So, I picked up Kate about ten minutes after school started."

"Oh. And, Cole?" I asked.

"I WENT TOO!" He screamed, and turned around. I realized why he was yelling. He was using my earphones and he was trying to yell over the music.

"Hey, Cole! Give those back!" I ran over and snatched them. "Don't take my stuff."

He started whining, and Mom said, "Please, Haylie, can't you be a little bit more generous with your stuff? I told Cole he could use them. Can't he use them for a little while longer?"

"No! They're mine!" I said, "He can save up and buy his own if he wants, I don't care!"

"Haylie! You will let him use the earphones, and you will learn to be nicer and less firm with your siblings!" she snapped. "Never in my childhood would I do something as bad as mouth off to my siblings, because I knew darn well I would get knocked flat if they told my mother!"

"Sorry Mom, but… they are mine. I did buy them with my own money."

"Yes, but there is such a thing called sharing!"

"Yeah. Sharing!" Cole mimicked. And he did some sort of weird puppy face that didn't look cute at all.

"Fine. But, if you don't give 'em back, I'm going to go into your room and steal them right off your earlobes, got me?"

"FINE!" And he sobbed into a pillow.

"Haylie, don't be so harsh with him!"

"AGH!!!!!!!!! This is so frustrating! I SAID HE COULD USE THEM!!!" I screamed, which only made Cole cry louder and harder.

"Haylie, I want you to really think about how you've been acting, lately. I'm not too happy with you. And, if you do it again, I will have to erase your privilege of paying for one of your sports. You want to do it, you pay for it on your own," Mom said.

"But, Mom!" I screeched.

"I said this is your second strike. One more, Haylie, one more…" she said.

"You are not fair, sometimes!" I ran up to my room. Honestly, I didn't know what had gotten into me. I never acted like this! But, of course, Cole shouldn't have gone in my room and stolen them! But, Mom said yes, so he probably thought it was okay. Well, Cole still knew, probably, that it was not good to steal. Mom also should have known that I bought the headphones with my own money, and if Cole breaks them, he buys me a new pair.

And that was that.

Chapter Eighteen

ABOUT AN HOUR LATER, KEVIN came in my room. "Mom told me I needed to make some money – maybe do yard work. Can you do it for
me?"

"No, Kevin. Do your own work."

"I'll pay you," he grinned. "Come on in, Kristy,"

"Please? Kev and I want to go out today. We're going to visit Hollywood,"
Kristy pleaded.

"Why Hollywood?" I groaned.

"We want to see famous people!" She exclaimed.

"Oh."

"So, will you?" Kevin asked.

"How much are you paying me?" I asked.

"What's your minimum?" he asked.

"Twenty," I said.

"Cents?" Kristy gasped.

"No. Dollars," I said.

"That's your minimum?" he exclaimed. His eyes widened. "You're gonna wipe
me out!"

"Shhh. You don't want me to tell Mom you're going out tonight... do you?" I asked.

"No!" Kevin hissed.

I grinned. "Okay. Twenty dollars."

I held out my hand. "Come on."

"Aw, Haylie!" he said.

"Mom!" I screamed downstairs.

"Yes!?"

"No! Okay, here."

I smiled. "Nothing," I yelled downstairs.

He felt around in his pocket and fished out a twenty-dollar bill that had, "In God We Trust" written across the top. I held it up to the sun to see if it was a real twenty. It was. I said, "Okay, thanks," And they walked out.

"Yes!" I totally scammed him. I'm so evil.

But... he won, too. I had to work. Ugh.

So, I told Sabrina to cover for me. "Sabrina! Can you cover for me?"

"What?"

"I did it for you!"

"Oh, fine. What are you doing?" she asked. "Going out with Seth!?"

"No!" I hissed. "And shut up. You'll get me in trouble."

There was a minute if silence.

"So... remember when you covered for me?" she said.

"Yeah," I groaned. I knew where this was going.

"Well, I paid you. So, now you pay me," she took a rubber band off her wrist and tied her hair into a bun with it.

"But——"

"I paid you! I'll take twenty, please," she said, picking at her nail polish. "Mom!" she yelled.

"No! Whatever," I took Kevin's twenty out of my jean pocket. "Here."

She smiled. "I knew it. I mean, honestly, who would Mom believe, me? Or you?"

"You," I groaned. "But Dad would believe me! He thinks I'm the most innocent person ever!"

"Prove it! I need an example," she glared at me. "Sometime this day! Hurry up!" She said while I was trying to think of an example.

"Shut up! I'm trying to think."

"Think faster!" She pinched me. "Hurry up!!!"

"Fine. For example: when we were watching the Super Bowl last time, I acted interested, so in the future, he would love me. And he does!"

"Fine, but Mom runs the house."

"Not true! Dad has just as equal part as Mom!" I said.

"Girls, what are you arguing about in there? I'm trying to work!"

"Fine. Sorry Mom!" I said. "I'm cleaning."

"You did this… you gave me twenty dollars to… clean!?"

"It's… complicated."

"Whatever, I got paid to see you work. I don't care: I've done my part," she sneered and walked out of the room.

So, technically, I have gained nothing. This was not my day. Was something going to happen and my day was going to brighten up? I thought about it, well, it happens in stories and fairy tales! I thought some more. But that's stories and fairytales. I doubted it.

Then, I thought, *If it happens to me, God, I'll pay you back. I'll… pray every night? Yeah. I should already do that, I know.* And, I knew it wouldn't happen, but there was a thought in my head… it was still confident.

When I tried to tell it that nothing was happening, Mom asked me if I was okay, because I was "talking to myself".

"I'm fine," I said. And, I wondered upstairs, and thought and thought some more. Why did it have to be such a secret? It didn't. I could get my money back from Sabrina… and tell Mom. "YES!" I said aloud. And, dashed downstairs. "Sabrina!"

"Room," she called, and I ran into her room.

"Um, I need my money back."

"What!?" her eyebrows rose.

"Um… the money…" I tried.

"I know 'what'. But why do you need your money back!? And… that doesn't mean I'm gonna give it back to you."

"Well, I decided to tell Mom."

Her eyebrows went back to normal, "Why."

"Um, I don't know… because it doesn't have to be a secret…?" I said. I didn't think I had the best chance in getting my money back. "Well?"

"Okay… only because I'm nice," she bit her lip.

"Yes! Thanks, Sabri—"

"Save it. There are strings attached," she smiles.

"Oh, no."

"Oh… yes," she snickered.

"So… what do you want?" I sighed.

"You will tell Mom about my… generosity."

"Fine… but… that's it?"

"Oh, no. Whoever said that?" she smiled and ran her fingers through her brown hair. "I want one hundred dollars."

"WHAT!?" I screamed.

"Oh, alright. It was worth a try. You will tell Mom. And… maybe she'll let me off at chores and stuff!"

"Fine. Can I go, now?"

"Yes."

"With… the money," I said.

"Eh, it was worth a try. Here you go… it must be somewhere in here…" She searched through her moneybox.

"Hey. I don't want the exact bill I handed to you!" I exclaimed.

"Good 'cause that would take a lot of time," she breathed a sigh of relief.

"Hurry!" I rushed her.

"Fine, here," she handed me a crumpled twenty-dollar bill.

"Thanks!" I rushed into the kitchen, "Mom!"

"Ooh!" She dropped a ladle into the soup she was stirring. "Honey, you scared me!" She said, retrieving her ladle.

"Sorry. I had to tell you something."

"Okay," she said, putting the ladle on a rag, and wiping her hands on a paper towel. "Go."

"Well, see Kev went out with Kristy went out and asked me if I would do his chores," I explained, gestured with my hands.

"Oh!" She gasped. "Honey!!! Come here," she yelled to my dad.

"What? Honey, you say something?" my dad called from the living room.

"No, Dad, she said... nothing!" I yelled back.

There was no reply.

"Well, what was that for?" My mom stared at me.

"Nothing. Just... listen."

She nodded and signaled that she was zipping up her lips.

"So, I said I would... for twenty dollars. And, I asked Sabrina to cover for me, and she asked me for twenty dollars. I paid her, and was left with nothing. And, I just wanted to tell you that I got my money back from Sabrina and Kevin is still gone before I left," I said, in a couple short breathes.

"Okay... so what do you want me to do? Ground Kevin? Make him do his chores? Leave it as it is?" she asked.

"Uh, I dunno," I said, shrugging.

"Well, make up your mind. This soup isn't going to stir itself. And these dishes aren't going to wash themselves. And this kitchen isn't going to clean itself up after I cook. See? I've got lots of work to do around the house, Haylie," she smiled. "I think you should keep your part of the bargain and do your yard work."

"Why! You choose to agree with Kevin now," I say.

"Well, only because he's right this time. He paid you to do yard work, you should do yard work. That's the only logical thing I can think of. I have to agree with him. If I agreed with you, it would mean I would be saying that you don't have to do the work you're getting paid for. That's not right."

"But, Mom! This is different!!!"

"In what way?" she smiled. "If you get paid, you should do the work!"

"Fine," I said. I knew she was right, but I really did NOT want to work.

Thirty minutes later...

Elizabeth called my house and asked me if I wanted to go rollerblading.

I said I would.

When I got there, we headed out. Which probably not too smart, because it was a hill… and Sheba, her dog, was coming.

Elizabeth held Sheba's leash, and I skated extra fast.

Sheba saw me, and we went SO fast, I swear!

When we went inside her house (with multiple bruises, each) her dad said, "What happened to you guys?"

We laughed and her dog knocked both of us down.

We had a little spazzum. (I'm not even sure that's a word. But, the point is that we spazzed.) (That's not a word either)

When I got home, I collapsed onto my bed. "Ohhh," I moaned, and rubbed my sore leg.

And… I fell asleep.

And I had a dream.

It was me and all of my friends by our pool, laughing and talking. Having a good time. I bolted up, and I knew to start making the invitations immediately.

```
Dear friends,
PARTY!
```

About KidPub Press

KidPub is devoted to helping kids develop their writing skills by giving them a safe, fun, supportive place to express their creativity. At KidPub we understand that kids have great ideas and plenty of stories to tell.

In addition to our web site, we publish books, like this one, written by kids of all ages. You can find many more books to enjoy, written by young authors, in our online bookstore at http://bookstore.kidpub.com.

Thousands of visitors come each day to KidPub to read the stories posted by our members, and to post their own writing. We invite you to visit KidPub, browse our books, read new stories, and find out how you can publish your own book with KidPub Press. We're on the web at www.kidpub.com.

Made in the USA
Monee, IL
05 April 2020